PENGUIN BOOKS

GRAND UNION

'The stories in *Grand Union* address both eternal existential queries and decidedly contemporary concerns' *Financial Times*

'Tackles subjects including cancel culture, desire and race with Smith's trademark insight and lightness of touch' *Stylist*

'A virtuoso performance' BBC

'A gorgeous mix of genres and perspectives' *New York Post*

'Acute observation, humour and warmth . . . A startling, energizing collection from a writer unafraid to take risks' *i*

'An exuberant volume that's bracing, thoughtful and frequently very funny' *Mail on Sunday*

'Provocative, incisive and revealing Smith's prodigious talent, which she refuses to limit to any singular genre or subject . . . Offering sly commentary on the lives we live today, and what might be in store for our futures' *NYLON*

'Smith offers sharp social commentary in this wry collection of stories that takes on the complications of the modern world' *Psychologies*

'A set of sharp, savvy tales which juggles genres, brims with vitality and lays bare hearts and minds. She does what all good writers should do: leaves her reader wanting more' *Herald*

By the same author

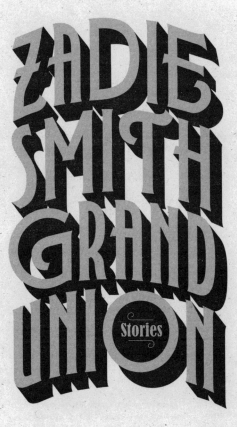

ZADIE SMITH

GRAND UNION

Stories

PENGUIN BOOKS

PENGUIN BOOKS

UK | USA | Canada | Ireland | Australia
India | New Zealand | South Africa

Penguin Books is part of the Penguin Random House group of companies
whose addresses can be found at global.penguinrandomhouse.com

First published by Hamish Hamilton 2019
Published in Penguin Books 2020
001

The permissions on pp. 245–246 constitute an extension of this copyright page

Typeset by Jouve (UK), Milton Keynes
Printed and bound in Great Britain by Clays Ltd, Elcograf S.p.A.

A CIP catalogue record for this book is available from the British Library

ISBN: 978–0–241–98312–6

www.greenpenguin.co.uk

Penguin Random House is committed to a
sustainable future for our business, our readers
and our planet. This book is made from Forest
Stewardship Council® certified paper.

For Maud

How can anyone fail to be

– 'Yesterday Down at the Canal', Frank O'Hara

CONTENTS

The Dialectic

'I would like to be on good terms with all animals,' remarked the woman, to her daughter. They were sitting on the gritty beach at Sopot, looking out at the cold sea. The eldest boy had gone to the arcade. The twins were in the water.

'But you are not!' cried the daughter. 'You are not at all!'

It was true. What the woman had said was true, in intention, but what the girl had said was true, too, in reality. The woman, though she generally refrained from beef, pork and lamb, ate – with great relish – many other kinds of animals and fish, and put out flypaper in the summer in the stuffy kitchen of their small city apartment and had once (though her daughter did not know this) kicked the family dog. The woman had been pregnant with her fourth child, at the time, and temperamental. The dog seemed to her, at that moment, to be one responsibility too many.

'I did not say that I am. I said that I should *like* to be.'

The daughter let out a cruel laugh.

'Words are cheap,' she said.

Indeed, at that moment the woman held a half-eaten chicken wing in her hand, elevated oddly to keep it from being covered in sand, and it was the visible shape of the bones in the chicken wing, and the tortured look of the thin, barbecued skin stretched across those bones, which had brought the subject to mind.

'I dislike this place,' said the daughter, definitively. She was glaring at the lifeguard, who had once again had to wade into the murk to tell the only bathers – the girl's own brothers – not to go past the red buoy. They weren't swimming – they could not swim. There were no waters in the city in which to take lessons, and the seven days they spent in Sopot each year was not long enough to learn. No, they were leaping into the waves, and being knocked over by them, as unsteady on their feet as newborn calves, their chests grey with that strange silt which fringed the beach, like a great smudge God had drawn round the place with a dirty thumb.

'It makes no sense,' continued the daughter, 'to build a resort town around such a filthy and unwelcoming sea.'

Her mother held her tongue. She had come to Sopot with her own mother and her mother had come with her mother before that. For at least two hundred years people had come here to escape the cities and let their children run wild in the public squares. The silt was of course not filth, it was natural, though no one had ever told the woman exactly what form of natural substance it was. She only knew to be sure to wash out all their costumes nightly in the hotel sink.

Once, the woman's daughter had enjoyed the Sopot sea and everything else. The candyfloss and the shiny, battery-operated imitation cars – Ferraris and Mercedes – that you could drive willy-nilly through the streets. She had, like all children who come to Sopot, enjoyed counting her steps as she walked out over the ocean, along the famous wooden board-walk. In the woman's view, the best thing about a resort town such as this was that you did whatever everybody else did, without thinking, moving like a pack. For a fatherless family, as theirs now was, this collective aspect was the perfect camouflage. There were no individual people here. In town, the woman was on the contrary an individual, a particularly unfortunate sort of individual, saddled with four fatherless children. Here she was only another mother buying candyfloss for her family. Her children were like all children, their faces obscured by huge clouds of pink spun sugar. Except this year, as far as her daughter was concerned, the camouflage was of no use. For she was on the very cusp of being a woman herself, and if she got into one of those ludicrous toy cars her knees would touch her chin. She had decided instead to be disgusted with everything in Sopot and her mother and the world.

'It's an aspiration,' said her mother, quietly. 'I would like to look into the eye of an animal, of any animal, and be able to feel no guilt whatsoever.'

'Well, then it has nothing to do with the animal itself,' said the girl pertly, unwrapping her towel finally and revealing her precious, adolescent body to the sun and the gawkers she now believed were lurking everywhere, behind every corner. 'It's just about you, as usual. Black again! Mama, costumes come in different colours, you know. You turn everything into a funeral.'

The little paper boat that had held the barbecue chicken must have blown away. It seemed that no matter how warm Sopot became there would always be that north-easterly wind, the waves would be whipped up into 'white horses' and the lifeguard's sign would go up and there would never be a safe time to swim. It was hard to make life go the way you wanted. Now she waved to her boys as they waved at her. But they had only waved to get their mother's attention, so that now she would see them as they curled their tongues under their bottom lips and tucked their hands into their armpits and fell about laughing when another great wave knocked them over. Their father, who could very easily be — as far as anyone in Sopot was concerned — around the next corner, buying more refreshments for his family, had in reality emigrated, to America, and now fixed car doors onto cars in some gigantic factory, instead of being the co-manager of a small garage, as he had once had the good fortune to be, before he left.

She did not badmouth him or curse his stupidity to her children. In this sense, she could not be blamed for either her daughter's sourness or her sons' immaturity and recklessness. But privately she hoped and imagined that his days were brutal and dark and that he lived in that special kind of poverty she had heard American cities can provide. As her daughter applied what looked like cooking oil to the taut skin of her tummy, the woman discreetly placed her chicken wing in the sand before quickly, furtively, kicking more sand over it, as if it were a turd she wished buried. And the little chicks, hundreds of thousands of them, perhaps millions, pass down an assembly line, every day of the week, and chicken sexers turn them over, and sweep all the males into huge grinding vats where they are minced alive.

Sentimental Education

Back then, she unnerved men. But couldn't understand why, and sought answers from unreliable sources. Women's magazines – women themselves. Later, in midlife, she came to other conclusions. Lay on the grassy pavilion above the Serpentine café, admiring a toddler, her own son, as he waded in and out of the paddling pool. Suddenly her daughter appeared at her shoulder: 'You look at him like you're in love with him. Like you want to *paint* him.' This daughter had just emerged from the lido, she was covered in duckweed. The toddler wore a huge soggy nappy hanging behind him, hardening like clay. It was something to consider. In the river Christo had placed a flat-topped *mastaba*, eighty feet tall, formed from many red and purple oil barrels, set atop each other. Pedalos shunted round it. Bold women in wetsuits swam by. Seagulls perched on top of it, shitting. This was also meant to be something to consider. The clouds parted and the late summer sun embraced Christo's eternal house and everything else, even her daughter's furious green face. Both the women's magazines and the women had placed their emphasis on lack and error. The problem was you were 'missing' something. Now, a quarter of a century later, she saw that what had looked like a case of lack was in fact a matter of inconvenient surplus. A surplus of what? Can you have a surplus of self?

But it was true: she'd always thought of men as muses. Always treated them that way.

Darryl was the first to like it. He wasn't very tall. But so beautiful! He had the African backside she wanted for herself; he was compact and muscular all over. Adorable cock, nothing too dramatic, suitable for many situations. She liked it best when it pressed flat against his belly, pointing to a woolly line of hair that thread upwards and then spread in two soft plains over his symmetrical chest. His nipples were alive to the world, crazy about it, they were like an insect's quivering antennae. The only bit of her body like that was her brain. She especially admired the hair on his head, soft and even, with no sharp sides. Her own head had been completely shaved after years of abuse from hairdressers' chemicals. She was starting afresh, trying to make it grow thicker, hoping to revive the African roots, but no one in that small college town had seen anything like it and she became an inadvertent sensation. But he knew.

'Have you met Darryl yet?'

'But you should meet Darryl! Oh my God you've got to!'

The college as an organism was adamant that they meet. They were two of only four black faces on campus. 'Darryl, Monica. Monica, Darryl! Finally!' They tried to be offended but the truth was they were grateful for any facilitation, being shy. They sat with their legs hanging over the water and discovered they'd grown up in the same postcode, ten minutes from each other, without ever meeting, and had been offered similarly low conditional grades – she some Bs, he some Cs – to demonstrate how deserving they were or how little was expected of them or how liberal the college was. It was hard to know. They both vaulted over this low bar, aceing everything. As social experiments they were unimpeachable.

They became aware that to the college, and on paper, they looked much the same. But they knew better. Street names, school names, the existence versus the absence of fathers. Glancing through the *Metro*, between Darryl's stop and her own – having not seen him in twenty-five years – she read a brutal news story and thought, yes, from my school emerged one England football player and two and a half pop stars; from Darryl's, this grinning loon who just decapitated someone in Iraq. On the other hand, the very first boy Monica ever kissed went on to stab a man to death in a chip shop around the same time she was fixing a mortar board to her head. Between Darryl's stop and her own she wondered lazily about what her life might have been had she married Darryl, or that murderous boy, or no one at all. Probably her husband had his own dull map of roads not travelled. You grow conventional in middle life. Choices made over time present themselves as branches running off the solid oaks that line the overground route to Kensal Rise. You grow grey, and thick in the hips. Yet, on happier days, she saw the same small, high breasts, the same powerful long legs, the familiar and delicious brown animal looking back at her, almost never ill and very strong. How much of this was reality? How much delusion? This was the question of the age, as far as she could tell. And the difference between now and being twenty was she was never sure, not from one moment to the next. Next stop Canonbury. Next stop menopause and no more denim. Or was it? Blind worms churning mud through their bodies is a better metaphor for what happens than roads not taken or branches un-sprouted. But no metaphor will cover it really. It's hopeless.

Six months prior to meeting Darryl, when she was still in London, she spent an interesting summer with a six-foot-six photographer's assistant, a white boy from Brixton, ex-skateboarder, who had once been a big name in tagging. There was a Bakerloo train that had one of his purple dragons sprayed down one side. She discovered an irrational admiration for very tall people. Kneeling in front of him felt like a form of worship. One day they were in the bath and she told a lot of jokes, and made him laugh, but like a comedian kept pursuing further laughs, with an increasingly heavy hand, and receiving less return for her efforts: quieter laughter, sighs. She changed tack. Three paragraphs on his ice-blue eyes, and Leni Riefenstahl haircut, and nine-inch, uncut penis. In the spirit of experiment, she went underwater and headed towards him with her mouth open. He got out of the bath and went home and didn't call for a few days and then wrote a very high-minded letter about being compared to a Nazi. A letter! Arriving in college, she had this cautionary example in mind. Don't talk about them like they're objects, they don't like it. They want to be the subject in all situations. Don't *you* try and be the subject. And don't try to make them laugh and don't tell them they're pretty.

*

All these rules had to be adapted for Darryl. He loved to laugh and delighted in physical worship. There was no aggression in him. He lay back and waited to be adored. The easy way she took him into her body, for example, painlessly, subsuming him, providing him with temporary shelter, until it came time to release him. But it was the nineties: the language was not on her side. You didn't 'release' men, they 'pulled out'. They were the subject. It had become normal to hear them mouthing off in the pubs, thrilled with the new licence to speak sex aloud: 'I rammed it right up her' or 'I fucked her in the arse.' But with Darryl, Monica discovered that this was just talk, masculine bravado, and in fact the largesse was all the other way around. One afternoon, after they had fucked all the way through the time allotted for morning lectures, she tried out the idea on him:

'In a matriarchy, you'd hear women boasting to their mates: "I subsumed him in my anus. I really made his penis disappear. I just stole it away and hid it deep inside myself until he didn't even exist."'

Darryl was cleaning himself with a tissue at the time, frowning at the brown stains. He stopped and laughed, but then lay back on her sperm-stained blue futon and frowned again, taking the notion seriously (he was studying Social Political Science).

'"I really swallowed him up,"' Monica continued, getting louder, without meaning to, '"I took his flesh and totally nullified it with my own flesh."'

'Yeah . . . I'm not sure it'll catch on.'

'But it should! It would be NICE.'

Darryl rolled on top of her, no taller and no shorter, and kissed her all over her face.

'You know what would be even nicer?' he said. 'If there was no matriarchy *or* patriarchy and people just said: "Love joined our bodies together and we became one."'

'Don't be disgusting,' she said.

There is an old cliché about street life: you leave, the streets follow. In Darryl's case, this was literal. Monica – who had nothing to do with the streets except living in them – had brought with her only a few pictures, a potted plant, and a fake Senufo stool her mother picked up in a Kenyan airport. Darryl had brought Leon, a third-generation Irish petty criminal from South Kilburn. Not in spirit, or metaphorically, but in person – he was living in Darryl's college room, on an airbed Darryl deflated each morning and hid in a suitcase so the cleaning ladies wouldn't find it. It was a strange arrangement, but the oddest thing about it, in Monica's view, was that Darryl didn't find it strange. He and Leon did everything together; they'd been friends since they were three. Attended the same local nursery and primary schools, and then on to the same secondary. Now they were going to be undergraduates together. Irrespective of the fact that Leon had failed all his GCSEs, had no A levels, and was not enrolled at the university.

Very quickly Monica realized that any relationship with Darryl must also be one with Leon. The two friends ate together, drank together, punted together, even studied together – in the sense that Darryl went to the library and Leon sat next to him, feet up on a desk, listening to *Paul's Boutique* on his MiniDisc player. The only time Monica had Darryl to herself was when she was nullifying his flesh in her flesh, and that was often over for only a few minutes before they heard Leon's hearty beatboxing at the door – his 'secret signal'. Darryl and Monica had then to get dressed, and the three of them would adjourn: to the college bar, to the river to get high, to the roof of the chapel to get higher.

'But it ain't like I don't pay my own way, though,' said Leon in response to Monica, one night when she was high enough to imply that he was taking advantage of her lover's sweet nature. 'I do my fucking bit, don't I?'

No one could say he didn't. He supplied the whole college with weed, Es and mushrooms when they were available, and what he liked to call 'the cheapest coke this side of the M4'.

Leon wore Kappa tracksuits on rotation. On especially cold days, a neon yellow Puffa and a furry Kangol cap were added. On hot days, he kept the bottom half of the tracksuit and paired it with a tight wifebeater that revealed a taut, wiry, ghost-white frame. He wore his vintage British Knights no matter the weather: he bought them from Japan, before the Internet, when this was not an easy thing to do. He did not look like anyone else yet at the same time did not stand out: his was a conventional face, not unpleasant to look at, neither handsome nor ugly. Short blonde hair, rigid with gel, blue eyes, a diamond stud in his left ear. He was the embodiment of the phrase 'white youth' when used in a police report. He could steal your car in front of you and you still wouldn't be able to identify him in a line-up. And yet, by the end of that first Michaelmas term, he was known by all, well loved. Some people can 'talk to anyone'. In a context where everybody was trying to be somebody – hoping to impress, developing a persona – his consistency was admired. He spoke the same way to the posh girls, the choral scholars, the nat-sci Northerners, the working-class maths geniuses, the two African princes, the ex-Territorial Army college porters, the Jewish North London intellectuals, the South American Marxist graduates, the lady chaplain, and – when the shit finally hit the fan – to the Provost himself. Part of his appeal was that he offered a vision of college life free from the burden of study. All those fantasies from the prospectus, on which the students had been sold – images of young people floating down stream or talking philosophically in high grass – that life had come true only for Leon. From the stained-glass panopticon of the library, Monica would spot him down there, at his liberty: lying on the Backs blowing smoke into the face of a cow, or in a punt with a crowd of freshers and bottle of cava. Meanwhile she wrote and rewrote her thesis on eighteenth-century garden poetry. All Monica's life was work.

In the evenings, she was hard at work again, trying to establish if the G-spot was a real thing or an ideological chimera of seventies feminism. With her index finger she could feel, deep inside, a sort of penny-sized raised area, facing outwards towards the stomach wall, and the idea was if she sat on Darryl and wrapped her legs around him very tightly and he did the same and they both stayed upright, moved rhythmically and listened to Foxy Brown, then the question might be finally resolved. But Leon was on her mind.

'Inside these gardens – these formal gardens – they'd have a hermit figure. In a grove, or at the centre of a maze. He was real, like a real homeless man, and he just sort of sat there being at liberty, while the house and gardens were all about hard work, about labour and capital. He was the light relief. And I think Leon's basically like that hermit.'

'I really don't want to talk about Leon right now.'

'And when these posh girls are shagging him, it's like Lady Whoever coming out of the great house to patronize the hermit.'

'I think Leon's more like the Lord of Misrule. Or the college duppy. Him pale like duppy!'

'Ugh – I'm suddenly too hot.'

'Gal, you know mi like dem fih sweat? You sweat like big woman!'

'Big Woman*ist*. Seriously, I need to get off – I'm too hot.'

'I thought we were looking for your secret garden? I was going to write it up for Nancy Friday. You're letting the side down.'

A joke, but she still remembered it.

It was very important to Monica that Leon get caught. She never said this aloud, or admitted it to Darryl, but she felt it. Despite her youth, she was secretly on the side of law and order. At first, she put her hope in the cleaning ladies – the 'Bedders' – but they discovered the subterfuge within weeks and never reported it. Monica walked into the communal kitchen one morning and found Leon sat up on the counter, having a cup of tea with a couple of them, gossiping away, sharing a breakfast fag. Very convivial. All Monica ever got from the Bedders was silence and contempt. They tended to be Irish ladies of a certain age who hated their work, and the lazy, entitled, usually filthy students for whom they cleaned. They did not see why passing a few poxy exams meant anyone deserved to sit around for three years doing what appeared to be fuck all at the taxpayer's expense. But Monica was very committed to the idea of a meritocracy – it was the fundamental principle undergirding her life. Some part of her always expected any nearby adults to be spontaneously applauding her efforts in all areas. She urgently wanted the Bedders to love her, and to express class allegiance with her, for her own grandmother was a kind of bedder: she emptied the bedpans at St Mary's Hospital. Monica tried very hard not to give these put-upon ladies any extra work or make unnecessary requests. But sometimes it was unavoidable. In the summer term, when the sweet, rotten smell in her room had become impossible to ignore, she timidly asked her Bedder whether she could help solve the mystery of The Smell. Did she perhaps think, as Darryl did, that there might be a dead mouse somewhere in the fabric of the wall?

'Excuse me, do I look like bloody Columbo?'

It was different with Leon. The Bedders knew for certain he was absolutely undeserving and for this very reason they loved him. He'd no better marks than their own kids, after all, and yet he was *here*, and simply by continuing to live in the black fella's room – and getting away with it – he demonstrated there was nothing special about these stuck-up little twats who thought they ruled the world. They baked him homely treats and advised him on his love life:

'See, Marlene, the thing is, she keeps turning up at my door. I mean, Darryl's door.'

'Well, I heard she's the second cousin of Princess Diana, if you can believe that.'

'Posh birds are always the randiest.'

'They're certainly the worst behaved. I'll tell you this: we all think you could do better, Leon, no messing.'

'Marlene, are you chatting me up?'

'Oh, go on with you!'

'You're old enough to be my mum, Marlene, you do know that?'

They were trying a new thing where he came in little white spirals on her chest and then he had to lick it off. More work. But the only thing she gleaned from it was that she liked the idea more than the feeling of cold cum on her chest. And Leon was still on her mind.

'What are you going to do about him?'

'About him how?'

'Sooner or later, he's going to get caught and you'll both be sent down.'

'You're allowed friends to visit.'

'He's been "visiting" for nine months.'

'Don't you like Leon?'

'I don't like the idea of a young white man dragging a young black man down into the mud. It's utterly grotesque.'

'Utterly grotesque' was one of the new phrases she'd picked up in college.

'"A young black man"? "Hello, I'm Darryl, nice to meet you. I'll be licking the cum off your tits today."'

'You know what I mean.'

'Monica, I wouldn't *be* here without Leon.'

'Oh my God what are you talking about!'

Then he said something she couldn't understand.

'He has faith in me.'

She often heard parents comparing their small children to Nazis and fascist dictators but in her experience the correct analogy was the Stasi, or really any secret police. Their greatest pleasure was informing on each other. Sometimes she would walk into the house after work and a child would fly at her with a passion far beyond affection, lit up with the desire to tell her that the other one had done something terrible. What followed never made sense: automatically she said: 'Don't tell tales,' but then in the next beat requested more information; then, over hysterical protests, had to condemn the act and the reporting of it simultaneously, while all the time pretending that she was an almighty judge who had never in her life either committed a crime or informed on a criminal. But whenever her daughter's lovely mouth quivered with the almost erotic delight of exposure she was sent back to a memory of herself, with much the same expression on her face, slipping an anonymous note under the Provost's door.

Two days after she did it, Leon was gone. No one knew it was her, and no one suspected, least of all Darryl. He clung to her like she was the life ring, never knowing she'd sunk the ship. She'd imagined of course that he'd be sad about Leon, but it turned out she had not imagined sufficiently. The effect was shocking. He stopped going to lectures, stopped doing much of anything, and refused to accompany her to any social thing, even to the bar downstairs. She began to feel like that government doctor separating Elliott from E.T. He seemed to be withering – his whole world shrank. Now it consisted only of her. Fuck, eat, smoke, repeat. The mouse fumes and the weed fumes and the sex fumes. A day would come when she would wish she had a bottle of that scent, could take a big, fortifying sniff: *ah, 1995* . . . But when it was happening it was hideous. He just wanted to be with her, all the time. It was unnatural. If she mentioned a party, he'd lose his temper:

'Why d'you want to hang out with those people?'

'*Those* people are our friends.'

'We don't have friends here. These people are from a different world.'

'It's the world we live in.'

'We live in love.'

But it was ridiculous that they were in love! They were nineteen! What were they going to do: just *stay* in love all through college and perhaps even beyond, two people who had grown up practically right next door to each other? Just stick it out all the way to the end, *à la* some pre-Freudian Victorian novel? Thus missing a myriad of sexual and psychological experiences along the way? That was literally crazy!

'It's not *literally* crazy. Mum's been with Dad since they were fifteen. She had me when she was seventeen!'

'Darryl, your mum stacks shelves at *Iceland*.'

But how had she let that come out of her mouth!

In the months that followed their break-up she went to work, collecting sexual and psychological experiences. She spent some time treating a posh girl from Mumbai called Bunny like a muse, but this was less benign: a thick strain of unconscious misogyny ran through it, a cultural residue maybe, but passing specifically through Monica. She shocked herself one night, looking down at her own naked body to get a better view of Bunny, who was presently taking out Monica's tampon, by the string, with her teeth, while, unbeknownst to Bunny, Monica was thinking: *Yeah you take it out. Take it out, you little bitch.* Disgusted with herself, she broke it off, in the high-minded, youthful hope that sex and morality might one day perfectly align. Not long after that, she started spending a lot of time in the college bar, holding court, trying to start complicated drunken conversations about cultural theory with willing victims and then 'winning', by immediately disagreeing with anyone who aligned with her, like a knight in chess moving out of a rook's columnar range.

One night, five months later, she saw Leon. It was the night before the college ball, which was to be a sad sort of posh rave, featuring expensive Jungle DJs from London, mostly sourced by Leon and paid for by every Bedder's favourite sucker: The Great British Taxpayer. In a way, she was happy to see an old friend: she'd had a long, strange day, up to that point. That very morning, she'd risen from Bunny's bed with a whacking hangover – after an unfortunate bout of drunken, last-people-in-the-bar sex; then, after lectures, she knocked on Darryl's door, to see if they could 'find a way to be friends', although she knew, even as she was saying it, that this was not the reason she had come. He was stoned: resistance was futile. He giggled in the old way as she played with his nipples, but when it was over he turned icy cold. He went to his desk, sat down totally naked and opened a textbook. She thought it was a gag at first – but no. When she asked if she could hang around he said: 'You do what you like.' She got dressed and let herself out, offering no goodbyes and hearing none. That was at five. Since then, she'd been in the bar, drinking vodka and lime, each one taxpayer subsidized and so only one pound twenty. So far, she'd downed six. A little unsteadily she got to her feet and peered through the mullioned windows. It was Leon for sure. Standing next to the rising edifice of the pyramid stage presently being constructed by a small army of builders, right in the middle of the quad. She watched a huge speaker being hauled upright like a statue of Stalin. This must be the expensive sound system Leon himself had convinced the ball committee to secure, back in January, when Leon was still able to attend ball committee meetings. Now the prodigal son had returned. To witness the monument he had built. Also to sell Es.

When he walked in and sat down in her booth he had a very serious face. She felt judged, which was her least favourite thing in the world to feel. Did he know? Had he found out somehow? Oh God was it the *Iceland* thing?

'Mate, he was in *love* with you. And you just left him like it was nothing. You know you really hurt him? He was fucking destroyed! And that's my brother right there!'

She was astonished. In all the many stories she'd told herself about herself since childhood, the narrative that had never appeared, not in any form, was the one where she had the power to hurt anybody in any way. It was such an alarming sensation and so intolerable to her sensibility that she immediately bought some coke off Leon, did the coke, drank a lot more than she could handle, and flirted like a lunatic. Soon enough she was walking out of the bar with Leon, hand in hand, into the warm air.

'What are we doing?'

'Taking back the night. You're always banging on about it. Feminism. Now we're doing it.'

'That's not what that means.'

'Follow me.'

'What about Darryl?'

He raised his eyebrows, surprised. He had a new piercing in one of them, a little black bar, set slantwise, like the lines Monica drew in the margins of novels, next to the word SUBTEXT.

'No girl never broke us up, don't you worry.'

He held her hand and walked onto the grass. Normally neither student nor non-student were allowed to do this, but this evening they passed unnoticed among all the hard hats and orange safety vests. They crawled through a hole in the huge tarpaulin to the side of the stage. Sank down into the mud. She found herself utterly frantic for him.

'Calm down, calm down. Monica, you ain't gonner try and put something up me, are you? Cos I'm not about that.'

'*What?*'

And then she remembered. But it was unfair: there had once been a *hypothetical* conversation about strap-ons in the context of a *theoretical* conversation about Hélène Cixous. But she didn't want to penetrate any man, she wanted to subsume them. She felt wounded and annoyingly misidentified. Also, it proved what she'd long suspected: Darryl told Leon absolutely everything.

'No, I'm bloody not. Come here.'

From above came the noise of the workers labouring, hammering and nailing, creating surplus value for bloated plutocrats, while down below two anarchists, naked from the waist down, tried to fuck in the middle of the quad, protected from sight by their tarpaulin mausoleum. Monica could feel a cold trickle of coke going from her nose cavity down her throat, and the sense that this would all work better as anecdote than reality. Nothing fit right, every touch was wrongly placed or timed – she longed for Darryl. She longed for all the people in the world and also for the one person who would rescue her from all this longing. She tried to analyse it. What was the problem? It wasn't his face or his body or his gender or his class or his race. It was *the flow of energy*. Incredible. She had only just turned twenty, and yet she had alighted upon the answer everybody had been seeking since the very beginnings of cultural theory – yes, it had fallen to Monica to uncover it. *Sometimes the flow is just . . . wrong.* There were people to whom you wanted to abase yourself, and people you wanted to abase; there were people you wanted to meet on a flat playing field – which was called 'love', for capitalism's and convenience's sake – and people you really didn't know what to do with. Leon turned out to be in the latter category. She couldn't work with him. He was surplus value. He represented wealth for somebody, but not her.

Leon stopped what he was trying to do, rolled off her, pointed to the Kappa trademark on his sleeve, and sighed.

'Ying. Yang. Man. Woman.'

'Excuse me?'

'My nan says it's like dancing. You can't both lead.'

She crawled back to her room. She had a dream. She was standing in the grounds of a chateau, in a grand eighteenth-century garden. There were manicured hedges and borders and mazes and fountains and statues. Maybe there was a hermit but she didn't see him. In the centre of it all was a giant swimming pool. It was filled with young men, beautiful, of many races and eye colours and hair textures, but all perfectly formed. They were cavorting in the water, rising and falling like dolphins, while at the four corners, on four diving boards, some amongst their number were doing spectacular flips into the water. And it was while admiring these acrobatics that she noticed all their perfect forms had an aberration: each groin was covered with an envelope of shimmering, translucent skin, which contained and obscured whatever was within that pouch, as surely as Baryshnikov's white tights. In the dream, she reached into a pocket she apparently had and felt the presence of a little pocket knife and knew at once that this was her instrument: each pouch must be sliced.

It was good enough for Nancy Friday herself. Why did she wake up fearful? Not because the dream was perverse, exactly, but because she knew she would never forget it, and, by extension, the experiences that had led up to it. And she wanted to forget. In Monica's meritocracy, it was important not to keep memories: they only tied you to a past you were already preparing to abandon. She never consciously tried to remember anything. In dreams, it was different. A dream was a house your brain made without your permission, precisely to preserve memories and experiences and wayward impulses for all eternity, even the dead ones that only caused you pain, the ones from which you most wanted to be free. When she became a big woman she did sometimes wonder whether her daughter would ever experience such dreams, or if psychological contortions and self-surprises had simply ceased to exist, being outmoded like a MiniDisc player, or evolved beyond, like the appendix. The sorts of dream which, back then, if you had repeated it to anyone in college – even someone who knew you well and claimed to love you – they would only have smirked and said something like *Paging Dr Freud!* She never told a soul.

Could it be? Had she slept with three people in twelve hours? The things we put young bodies through! And because you can't remember forward, she would have to wait a long, long time to find a faint future echo of this extremity: breastfeeding one child, then a few hours later, lying next to another till it slept; then waking in a third room – all of this within one night – and pressing backwards into the beloved, to nullify his flesh in hers, and vice versa.

The Lazy River

We're submerged, all of us. You, me, the children, our friends, their children, everybody else. Sometimes we get out: for lunch, to read or to tan, never for very long. Then we all climb back into the metaphor. The Lazy River is a circle, it is wet, it has an artificial current. Even if you don't move you will get somewhere and then return to wherever you started, and if we may speak of the depth of a metaphor, well, then, it is about three feet deep, excepting a brief stretch at which point it rises to six feet four. Here children scream – clinging to the walls or the nearest adult – until it is three feet deep once more. Round and round we go. All life is in here, flowing. Flowing!

Responses vary. Most of us float in the direction of the current, swimming a little, or walking, or treading water. Many employ some form of flotation device – rubber rings, tubes, rafts – placing these items strategically under their arms or necks or backsides, creating buoyancy, and thus rendering what is already almost effortless easier still. Life is struggle! But we are on vacation, from life and from struggle both. We are 'going with the flow'. And having entered the Lazy River we must have a flotation device, even though we know, rationally, that the artificial current is buoyancy enough. Still, we want one. Branded floats, too-large floats, comically shaped floats.

They are a novelty, a luxury: they fill the time. We will complete many revolutions before their charm wears off – and for a few lucky souls it never will. For the rest of us, the moment arrives when we come to see that the lifeguard was right: these devices are too large; they are awkward to manage, tiresome. The plain fact is that we will all be carried along by the Lazy River, at the same rate, under the same relentless Spanish sun, for ever, until we are not.

Some take this principle of universal flow to an extreme. They play dead – head down, limbs limp, making no effort whatsoever – and in this manner discover that even a corpse goes round. A few people – less tattooed, often university educated – make a point of turning the other way, intent upon thrashing out a stroke against the current, never advancing, instead holding their place, if only for a moment, as the others float past. It's a pose: it can't last long. I heard one man with a fashionable haircut say he could swim the whole length backward. I heard his hipster wife dare him to do it. They had time for such games, having no children. But when he turned and made the attempt he was swept away within the minute.

The Lazy River is a metaphor and at the same time a real body of artificial water, in an all-inclusive hotel, in Almería, somewhere in southern Spain. We do not leave the hotel except to buy flotation devices. The plan is to beat our hotel at its own game. What you do is you do this: you drink so much alcohol that your accommodation is effectively free. (Only the most vulgar among us speak this plan aloud but we are all on board.) For in this hotel we are all British, we are en masse, we are unashamed. We enjoy one another's company. There is nobody French or German here to see us at the buffet, rejecting paella and swordfish in favour of sausages and chips, nor anyone to judge us as we lie on our loungers, turning from the concept of literature toward the reality of sudoku. One of our tribe, an older gentleman, has a portrait of Amy Winehouse on each shin, and we do not judge him, not at all, how could we? We do not have so many saints of Amy's calibre left to us; we cherish her. She was one of the few who expressed our pain without ridiculing or diminishing it. It is therefore fitting that in the evenings, during the brief spell in which we emerge from the Lazy River, we will, at karaoke hour, belt out her famous torch songs — full-throated, already drunk — content in the know-ledge that later, much later, when all of this is over, these same beloved verses will be sung at our funerals.

But karaoke was last night; tonight we have a magician. He pulls rabbits from places, unexpected places. We go to sleep and dream of rabbits, wake up, re-enter the Lazy River. You've heard of the circle of life? This is like that. Round and round we go. No, we have not seen the Moorish ruins. Nor will we be travelling into those bare, arid mountains. Not one soul among us has read the recent novel set right here, in Almería, nor do we have any intention of doing so. We will not be judged. The Lazy River is a non-judgement zone. This does not mean, how-ever, that we are blind. For we, too, saw the polytunnels — from the coach, on the way in from the airport — and we saw the Africans who work here, alone or in pairs, riding their bicycles in the merciless sun, moving between the polytunnels. Peering at them, I leaned my head against the shuddering glass of my window and, as in the fable of the burning bush, saw instead of the Africans a mirage. It was a vision of a little punnet of baby tomatoes, wrapped in plastic. Floating just outside my window, in the almost-desert, among the Moorish ruins. Familiar in aspect, it was as real to me as my own hand. And upon that punnet I saw a barcode, and just above that barcode was written *PRODUCT OF SPAIN – ALMERÍA*. The vision passed. It was of no use to me or anyone, at that moment, on our vacation. For who are we to – and who are you to – and who are they to ask us – and whosoever casts the first –

It's quite true that we, being British, could not point to the Lazy River on a map of Spain, but it is also true that we have no need to do so, for we leave the water only to buy flotation devices, as mentioned above. True, too, that most of us voted for Brexit and therefore cannot be sure if we will need a complicated visa to enter the Lazy River come next summer. This is something we will worry about next summer. Among us, there are a few souls from London, university educated and fond of things like metaphors and remaining in Europe and swimming against the current. Whenever this notable minority is not in the Lazy River, they warn their children off the endless chips and apply the highest-possible factor of suncream. And even in water they like to maintain certain distinctions. They will not do the Macarena. They will not participate in the Zumba class. Some say they are joyless, others that they fear humiliation. But, to be fair, it is hard to dance in water. Either way, after eating – healthily – or buying a flotation device (unbranded), they will climb back into the metaphor with the rest, back into this watery

Ouroboros, which, unlike the river of Heraclitus, is always the same no matter where you happen to step in it.

Yesterday the Lazy River was green. Nobody knows why. Theories abound. They all involve urine. Either the colour is the consequence of urine or is the colour of the chemical put in to disguise the urine or is the reaction of urine to chlorine or some other unknown chemical agent. I don't doubt urine is involved. I have peed in there myself. But it is not the urine that we find so disturbing. No, the sad consequence of the green is that it concentrates the mind in a very unpleasant way upon the fundamental artificiality of the Lazy River. Suddenly what had seemed quite natural – floating slowly in an unending circle, while listening to the hit of the summer, which itself happens to be called 'Slowly' – seems not only unnatural but surpassingly odd. Less like a holiday from life than like some kind of terrible metaphor for it. This feeling is not limited to the few fans of metaphor present. It is shared by all. If I had to compare it with something, it would be the shame that came over Adam and Eve as they looked at themselves and realized for the first time that they were naked in the eyes of others.

What is the solution to life? How can it be lived 'well'? Opposite our loungers are two bosomy girls, sisters. They arrive very early each morning, and instead of the common plastic loungers used by the rest of us they manage to nab one of the rare white four-poster beds that face the ocean. These sisters are eighteen and nineteen years old. Their outdoor bed sports gauzy white curtains on all four sides, to protect whoever lies upon it from the sun. But the sisters draw the curtains back, creating a stage, and lie out, perfecting their tans, often adjusting their bikini bottoms to check their progress, the thin line that separates brown stomach from pale groin. Blankly they gaze at their bare pubic mounds before lying back on the daybed. The reason I bring them up is that in the context of the Lazy River they are unusually active. They spend more time on dry land than anyone else, principally taking pictures of each other on their phones. For the sisters, this business of photographs is a form of labour that fills each day to its limit, just as the Lazy River fills ours. It is an accounting of life that takes as long as life itself. 'We both step and do not step in the same rivers. We are and are not.' So said Heraclitus, and so say the sisters, as they move in and out of shot, catching the flow of things, framing themselves for a moment: as they are, and as they are not. Personally, I am moved by their industry. No one is paying them for their labour, yet this does not deter them. Like photographers' assistants at real photo shoots, first they prep the area, cleaning it, improving it, discussing the angle of the light, and, if necessary, they will even move the bed in order to crop from the shot anything unsightly: stray trash, old leaves, old people. Prepping the area takes some time. Because their phones have such depth of image, even a sweet wrapper many yards away must be removed. Then their props are gathered: pink flower petals, extravagant cocktails with photogenic umbrellas protruding from them, ice creams (to be photographed but not eaten), and, on one occasion, a book, held only for the duration of the photograph and – though perhaps only I noticed this – upside down. As they prep, each wears a heart-breaking pair of plain black spectacles. Once each girl is ready to pose, she hands her glasses to her sister. It is easy to say they make being young look like hard work, but wasn't it always hard work, even if the medium of its difficulty was different? At least they are making a project of their lives, a measurable project that can be liked or commented upon. What are we doing? Floating?

A three-minute stroll from the back door of the hotel is the boardwalk, where mild entertainments are offered in the evenings, should we need something to do in the few darkling hours in which the Lazy River is serviced, cleaned, and sterilized. One of these entertainments is, of course, the sea. But once you have entered the Lazy River, with all its pliability and ease, its sterilizing chlorine and swift yet manageable currents, it is very hard to accept the sea: its abundant salt, its marine life, those little islands of twisted plastic. Not to mention its overfished depths, ever-warming temperature, and infinite horizons, reminders of death. We pass it by. We walk the boardwalk instead, beyond the two ladies who plait hair, onward a few minutes more until we reach the trampolines. This is the longest distance we have walked since our vacation began. We do it 'for the children'. And now we strap our children into harnesses and watch them bounce up and down on the metaphor, up and down, up and down, as we sit, on a low wall, facing them and the sea, legs dangling, sipping at tumblers of vodka, brought from the hotel, wondering if trampolines are not in the end a superior metaphor to lazy rivers. Life's certainly an up-and-down, up-and-down sort of affair, although for children the downs seem to come as a surprise – almost as a delight, being so outrageous, so difficult to believe – whereas for us, sitting on the wall, clutching our tumblers, it's the ups that have come to appear a little preposterous, hard to credit; they strike us as a cunning bit of misdirection, rarer than a blood-red moon. Speaking of which, that night there was a blood-red moon. Don't look at me: southern Spain has the highest ratio of metaphor to reality of any place I've ever known. There everything is in everything else. And we all looked up at the blood-red moon – that bad-faith moon of 2017 – and each man and woman among us understood in that moment that there is no vacation you can take from a year such as this. Still, it was beautiful. It bathed our bouncing children in its red light and set the sea on fire.

Then the time ran out. The children were enraged, not understanding yet about time running out, kicking and scratching us as we unstrapped them from their harnesses. But we did not fold, we did not give in; no, we held them close, and accepted their rage, took it into our bodies, all of it, as we accept all their silly tantrums, as a substitute for the true outrage, which of course they do not yet know, because we have not yet told them, because we are on holiday – to which end we have come to a hotel with a lazy river. In truth, there is never a good moment. One day they will open a paper or a web page and read for themselves about the year – 2050 or so, according to the prophets – when the time will run out. A year when they will be no older than we are now. Not everything goes round and round. Some things go up and –

On the way back to the hotel, we stop by the ladies who plait hair, one from Senegal and the other from the Gambia. With the moon as red as it is, casting its cinematic light, we can glimpse the coast of their continent across the water from our own, but they did not cross this particular stretch of ocean, because it is even more treacherous than the one between Libya and Lampedusa, by which route they came. Just looking at them you can tell that they are both the type who could swim the Lazy River backward and all the way round. In fact, isn't this what they have done? One is called Mariatou, the other Cynthia. For ten euros they will plait hair in cane rows or Senegalese twists or high-ridged Dutch braids. In our party, three want their hair done; the ladies get to work. The men are in the polytunnels. The tomatoes are in the supermarket. The moon is in the sky. The Brits are leaving Europe. We are on a 'getaway'. We still believe in getaways. 'It is hard in Spain,' Mariatou says, in answer to our queries. 'Very hard.' 'To live well?' Cynthia adds, pulling our daughter's hair, making her yelp. 'Is not easy.'

By the time we reach the gates of the hotel all is dark. A pair of identical twins, Rico and Rocco, in their twenties, with oily black curls and skinny white jeans – twin iPhones wedged in their tight pockets – have just finished their act and are packing up their boom box. 'We come runner-up *X Factor* Spain,' they say, in answer to our queries. 'We are Tunisia for birth but now we are Spain.' We wish them well and goodnight, and divert our children's eyes from the obscene bulge of those iPhones, the existence of which we have decided not to reveal to them for many years, or at least until they are twelve. At the elevators, we separate from our friends and their children and ascend to our room, which is the same as their room and everybody's room, and put the children to bed and sit on the balcony with our laptops and our phones, where we look up his Twitter, as we have every night since January. Here and there, on other balconies, we spot other men and women on other loungers with other devices, engaged in much the same routine. Down below, the Lazy River runs, a neon blue, a crazy blue, a Facebook blue. In it stands a fully clothed man armed with a long mop – he is being held in place by another man, who grips him by the waist, so that the first man may angle his mop and position himself against the strong yet somniferous current and clean whatever scum we have left of ourselves off the sides.

Words and Music

Went to the Vanguard last night, checked in on my other life.
She was sat on a stool, scatting, but it was like no scatting I ever
heard: she turned the sounds inside and out and backwards.
Instead of *la la do la be la* it was almost *al al od eb al* – like an
ululation. In fact, at times it sounded like she was just singing
that word, *ululation* over and over. Maybe she was. She sang in
Spanish, she sang in English, she made us laugh, she made us
cry, it was ridiculous! Everyone but me was over fifty and sort
of Anglo-Saxon-looking but she didn't let that stop her. She
reminded me why I'm not a singer. Same reason atheists whisper in church. Fred Hersch was on the piano – he walked up to
it on crutches and he left that way, too. I moved my chair so he
could get by. I wish music meant that much to me. Blessed are
those to whom music means that much.

Uptown, on 123rd Street, near Marcus Garvey Park, a Miss
Wendy English lowered herself into the same chair Stokely sat
in. It's not an imitation, it's not *like* that chair, it's the exact same
fucking chair, whether various museums realize it or not. This
is her sister's house. Her sister was once a Panther, which a lot of
the time meant it fell to her to organize stuff for men who were

big on rhetoric but low on practical detail. Certainly, none of them came by forty years later when Candice was alone, broke and dying. But the moral of this story is unclear because though Wendy was supposedly the good girl, never arming herself and only protesting civically, and though she married and moved to Boston and had three children who all attended four-year colleges, she is, this particular evening, as alone as Candice English ever was. No adult male made the distance. They're not dead, you understand – they're just otherwise occupied. New children, new countries, and so forth. Divorce, divorce, sudden disappearance, property dispute, in that order. This latest one, the property dispute, will surely be the last. He was too keen to get married, and whenever Wendy locked eyes with this seventy-two-year-old lothario, as he got down on one gabardined knee (he was always doing it) she saw her dead sister's brownstone right there in the centre of his shining black pupils. Miss Wendy herself is seventy-seven, nobody's fool. She recently broke off that last romance, retired from the library on a good pension, and moved back to New York City, to take possession of a house she hasn't visited since 1990. She sits in Candice's accidental gold mine and rips up the little postcards as they arrive, a few each week, the ones that explain how much the house is worth and how easy it would be to sell. She doesn't doubt it.

Many things have surprised Wendy about Candice's house. It isn't a mad woman's house, for one. Everything is very well organized. All the pictures of Wendy's children, which Wendy kept sending over the years, even after rational communication with her sister became impossible, these she found all neatly bound – along with their accompanying, unanswered letters – with sturdy elastic bands and stacked neatly in a series of box files. 'Don't send me any more of your shit – it goes straight in the trash and then I have to empty the trash.' But it wasn't true. She had kept it all, and lovingly. A lot of things turned out not quite to be as they had been presented. Madness might be a good way to stop people coming by. It had proved less shameful, possibly, to be mad, here in New York City, than to be lonely, or under-employed. For there was a time when Candice was at the centre of a hurricane. Yes, for at least a decade she was the eye of a terrific storm, and it must have been awful when all of a sudden that storm moved on, gave up the cause, ran out of funds, got thirty to life, and Candice found herself alone, looking out of this beautiful picture window, over at the park, where not even a breeze moves the ginkgos. Whereas Wendy, having had, comparatively speaking, much less drama in her life, is far more familiar with stillness, and silence – the textures of silence. Often, she sits in her sister's Stokely chair for precisely four minutes and thirty-three seconds and gets her John Cage on. She hears birds, she hears garbage trucks, she hears, *Hey, bitch, you better have my money!* The whole city symphony. She gets a lot out of that.

Another surprising thing: Candice's collection of vinyl. As sisters, they had not agreed on much, having such different temperaments, agreeing on freedom but not how to get it or what it might look like once you did – but they had a home in music. Fondest of all memories: grooving hand in hand, swaying, to Bootsy's 'I'd Rather Be With You', at a family barbecue, before the second man vanished and the kids grew old enough to be fearful of Aunt Candice and her habit of phoning up and reading terrifying stories from the newspaper into the receiver. They were two lithe little ladies back then, still in their forties, both with locks, for their hair often agreed where their heads did not.

Later they became tiny old birds and all that glorious hair turned to white fluff which Wendy alone had the sense to cut short. They thought of their mother who had the foresight to grow ever larger and more imperious with age. They regretted their Caribbean father's genes, which tended towards wiriness, and had damned Wendy at least to a decade of *please, please take my seat*.

Please kiss my ass. Don't need your seat — I got my own. And please stay away from this chair for it is an heirloom, a piece of living history, or else it is a thirty-buck copy my crazy sister picked up in a yard-sale somewhere. Never mind. Death converts everything to treasure, everything gets fixed in place so you can spray it in gold. Beethoven! Never had Candice breathed a word of Beethoven to Wendy and yet here it all was, and if Wendy had known about *that*, well, it might have been something they could have shared. Now she put on the 7th, the *Allegretto*, and imagined a golden alternative: two noble-looking old dames, long freed of useless men, walking down to the Lincoln Center to listen to this procession, this march through history, and hearing, in the counterpoint, their two different journeys, their highs and lows. Oh, that would have been something, really something, but it didn't happen that way, it didn't and it couldn't, because America is the kind of bitch who turns anyone who truly cares about Her into a crazy person.

Myron's kingdom stretches from one end of Bleecker to the other. He moves around it all day and late into the night, and no one knows where he sleeps, though of course nothing could be easier than asking him. His nemesis is the kerb. Some kerbs in this city are ludicrously high and as strong as he is in the upper body, sometimes he can't get the chair over these kerbs – especially if his plastic bags are full and hanging off the handlebars – so he waits wherever he is for someone to appear behind him and push. And as a piece of city choreography we all have this down to a fine art by now. One person takes over where the other left off and Myron doesn't even turn around to see who it is – he just knows us from the sound of our voices. Then, once you've got him over the kerb, there's the question of whether he wants company for a block or two. Usually he does. For a man without legs he talks a lot about dancing. Back in the day he was crazy about disco. Few people care for disco these days but Myron makes it sound like it was the music of the gods. We say to him, *Are you sure you're not just sentimental about disco because you had legs back then?* He thinks that shit is hilarious. He says, The thing you don't understand about disco is it's the only music in America that truly brought black and white folks together in the same room and then made them dance all night because those goddamn songs don't end! They just run into each other! They're like the life force itself! We don't agree, but we laugh along. Then he turns serious, he says, Well, it was a better time in America, that's for damn sure. We are not sure. Nixon? The Iran hostages? Jim Jones? The Fall of Saigon? Still, maybe he's right.

There's a joyful cipher under Washington Square Arch, most warm nights, starting around ten. I like it because it's inauthentic, like me. It's possible that there's nothing less real in this world than two black dudes, two Puerto Ricans and a white girl rapping under the stars of Greenwich Village, and yet there they are, you can poke them, they're not holograms. In my experience, the less claim a person has to a thing the harder they chase it, and these five are strivers all. Never saw anybody work so hard for a rhyme.

Three benches along sits Abraham Lincoln. Same beard, same face, and he's got an outfit that works. It's not a costume, exactly, but the general impression is that this is basically what Lincoln would wear if he were alive today and spent his days between MacDougal, Thompson and the park. I suppose he's crazy, but he's terribly solemn and dignified and he doesn't talk to himself or to anyone. He just strides around doing his Lincoln bit. In winter, he toughs it out as long as he can but come December you start to see him in a beanie and a large pea coat and L.L.Bean snow boots and I have to say the Lincoln effect is lessened somewhat. I really feel for him then. Not only because it's cold but because the weather is stripping him of his true self and that's a terrible thing to witness. For most of the winter he looks downhearted and ashamed, like a man forced to live in a body he doesn't recognize. However, he doesn't give the impression of owning any technology or even being aware of its existence, so he is at least saved the indignity of knowing that when you google his name the first thing that comes up is *What did Abraham Lincoln do that was so important?* Which is like hearing seven million fourth-grade foreheads smack onto their desks at once. Then winter thaws. Out pop the daffodils and the livelier rats, though spring is truly heralded by the appearance of our President, back doing his local rounds, in his stovepipe hat and his topcoat and that flash of black silk at the throat which pulls the whole look together. He doesn't speak in spring, no more than he does in winter, but I did once hear him sing. I was sitting under the cherry blossoms and he walked past, his voice very low and hard to hear, but if you happened to tune in to it, wow, it was really something beautiful:

Michael, row the boat ashore, hallelujah.
Michael, row the boat ashore, hallelujah.
Michael's boat is a music boat, hallelujah.

About two hours later I saw him sitting outside Wendy's eating a Wendy's. The spell was not broken. He who sings to himself without earbuds is especially precious to me now, like hearing the song of a bird long thought extinct.

Late in the summer, Dev played Central Park. Historically speaking, men with guitars have held their instruments in a certain way and pointed them at you like a penis and stood in the centre of whatever space and drawn all energy to them like a lightning rod stuck on a church spire. He didn't do any of that. For most of the show we had no idea where he was, really: he kept hiding behind other people, other instruments. He had his locks tied in a bun and wore some very high-waisted, salmon-coloured trousers. Meanwhile the crowd was filled with every type of true self imaginable in the Tri-state area. We all knew a great storm was coming. Because of technology, this storm could be predicted with extraordinary precision, so that as hot as it presently was, everybody knew for certain that it was going to rain on the stroke of ten o'clock. We felt the awesome power of knowing, we were high on it, and yet simultaneously I think we mourned the seers and witches and holy fools who used to try and divine these things from colours in the skies. In order to honour this ambivalent feeling, we stopped waiting for a show and began to understand we were at a seance. The music surrounded us. It was hot and heavy like the evening. It was a magical reversal of the technology: instead of iterations of Dev piping into all our bedrooms through our earbuds, now he had piped *us* into his small space, a strange sort of bedroom he had fashioned out of the park itself. We were all in it together. We had useless, transcendent thoughts like: *This, too, is America!* We were pretty high. But as I listened, I recalled a section of *Individuals: An Essay in Descriptive Metaphysics* by P. F. Strawson, in which he considers a purely auditory world, where there are no bodies, only sounds, and I could follow him as far as wondering whether if *I* were a sound, in a world of sounds, would I think of myself as a special item in the world of sounds, separate from them, and experience myself as a sound different from all the other sounds? Yet how would I think of myself as a separate item, a self that is experiencing sounds, when the sound I was making was only another item, aggregated, in this world of sounds? But then Strawson moves on, in the book, back to the ordinary world, hoping his reader will see the world afresh, and I confess I did not, I *do* not, I just see bodies everywhere, ascribing consciousness to themselves, because, well – because it really feels like your mind is inside your head! And it feels like your ears are connected to your soul! Yes, it does, whatever the philosophers say. Soul music! Given the state of the world none of us deserved what we got that night in Central Park but I can tell you we were terribly thankful for it. Then the rain came down hard and washed all this Manhattan tomfoolery into the drains.

Just Right

'And your father's in it?'

'Yes, ma'am. He helps my mother and makes the s– the –'

'The scenery? Try to breathe, Donovan, there's really no hurry. I'm sure you'll catch the others in the square.'

Miss Steinhardt sat on the very edge of her desk, working her nails with a bobby pin for the subway grime underneath.

'Now, Annette Burnham told me she went to see the show last weekend, with her mother and baby brother. Liked it a lot. And she said your father does the puppets, too – and you, too, isn't that right?'

'Oh. Yes, ma'am.'

'Don't call me ma'am, Donovan, we're not in the South. The things you kids get from television.'

'Yes, Miss St–' began Donovan, although he had neither an idea of the South, being Greenwich Village born and raised, nor much conception of television, which he was not allowed to watch. It was from his mother – whose father had been English – that he had received the strange idea that *ma'am* was a romantic form of British address, suitable for ladies you especially admired.

'Anyway, that's fine,' said Miss Steinhardt and looked over at the door until the boy had stopped wrestling with her name and closed his big wet mouth. 'Well, I'd say it's an unusual pastime for an eight-year-old. If I were you, I'd use it. Always best to use what you have.'

'Ma'am?'

'I'm sure the class would be interested to hear about it. You could bring in one of the puppets.'

'But –'

'Yes, Donovan?'

Miss Steinhardt moved one of her Mary Janes over the other and readjusted the long tartan skirt. She looked directly into the pale but not unbeautiful face: a long nose and bright green eyes, full, almost womanly lips, and a lot of dark hair, cut into a pair of slightly ludicrous curtains on either side of his narrow face. Really a boy who might have some hope of growing up into a Robert Taylor type – fine cheekbones, for a child – if it weren't for this absolute lack of purpose that revealed itself in every pore of his being.

'I already – g– g– got the pictures from the paper. I was planning on doing –' Donovan looked pleadingly at his teacher.

'Breathe, Donovan. It's not an interrogation. You're always in such a panic.'

'The museum, uptown. The one they've been building. They just st– started.'

'The Guggenwhatsit?'

Donovan nodded.

'Oh, well, yes, that would be fine,' said Miss Steinhardt, and wondered at the child, for she knew both G and S were the letters of his particular difficulty. She returned to her nails. Donovan, finely attuned to the moment when people grew bored of him, picked up his book bag and made his way out onto Sullivan Street, into Washington Square.

Lit by a bright fall sun, the arch looked more like its Roman progenitor than ever, and the boy found that when he walked into the leaves they made a pleasing crunch, and some wild man in the fountain was talking of Christ, and another stood on a bench singing about marijuana. His mother must never hear of his class assignment. He swore this solemnly to himself on Fifth Avenue, before walking as slowly as could be managed back to the mews. At that charming row of cottages he stopped and clutched a replica Victorian lamp post.

'Donovan? What are you, cracked? Get in here!'

Irving Kendal stepped out of their little blue home and took up a spot in the middle of the street. He packed a wad of tobacco into a pipe and peered over at his only son.

'Get in here. Hanging off that thing.'

The boy stayed put. It had recently come to his attention that his father's W came out like a V, that his H had too much water in it, and that everything he said came from another era.

'Who're you meant to be? Gene Kelly?'

Worse were the clothes: a broad-check three-piece suit in yellows and browns, cut to create the illusion of height, with widely spaced buttons and trouser legs that kicked madly at the knee. In the cottage next door, Donovan could see Miss Clayton in her elegant black-and-red kimono, standing at the window with her Maltese, Pablo, in her arms. She examined the father and then the son and gave the son a warm look of sympathy. It would be a fine thing to walk straight past Irving to go drink from Miss Clayton's soda-stream and listen to her bebop records, or sneak a look at the nude in her bathroom, or throw a beanbag around for Pablo to snap at with his harmless jaws. But such visits had to be rationed, out of loyalty. 'Four bedrooms, is it?' said Polly, if Donovan happened to visit the apartment of a friend with means. 'Well. I can see how you would have enjoyed that. Naturally. I know I would. Probably wouldn't want to come home at all.' Or: 'A soda-stream! Well, that's what disposable income means, I guess – not having anybody but yourself to dispose it *on*. But was it *deliciously* fizzy?' These conversations, much dreaded, always left Donovan with a free-floating sensation of guilt, all the less manageable for the indeterminacy of its source.

Now Polly emerged, barefoot despite the autumn chill. Donovan waved; his mother mimed her incapacity. In her left hand, she gripped a long piece of green velvet attached to a stake, held high to keep it from dragging on the ground, and in her right, three coloured feathers, each a foot long. Flying over to him, velvet streaming like the banner of a medieval princess, she moved with her toes pointed, so that what might simply be 'running' in another woman looked like a series of darting *pliés*.

'Just when I need you, darling – the whole of the forest has come away from the blocks. It'll need something better than glue this time – maybe tacks – and a whole new set of ferns from some very evergreen thing – it's of the utmost importance that it look lovely for Tuesday. Oh, Eleanor Glugel came by just after school and told me all about it and I think it's an excellent opportunity for the show, really excellent. I've been dying to talk to you about it – what took you so long? I had to listen to Glugel rattling on about her grandmother's tattoo for half an hour – that's what she's bringing in, to show – or tell – if you can believe it – her own grandmother.' Polly shuddered, and indicated a spot on the underside of her own delicate wrist: 'What an uplifting subject! Oh, but don't we all already *know* the world is full of horror? Do we *really* need to hear about it all the livelong day? There's no romance in that child whatsoever. No clue of the magic of storytelling. I'll bet you a dollar she wears a girdle already.'

All of this poured right into his ear, as Polly's lips were exactly level with it. She pressed his hand; he pressed back. She was perfect – an elf princess who had sworn allegiance only to him. Yet sometimes he wished that she could see, as he did, that theirs was a steely bond, not as easily broken as she seemed to imagine – one which he would never, ever give up, no matter how many four-bedroom apartments or soda fountains he came across in this life. Who else could make him agree to appear before his classmates in a pair of long johns, a nightshirt and a droopy hat with a bell on it? What larger sign of fealty could a knight offer a princess than his pride?

But the next morning Miss Steinhardt made a further announcement: the children were to work in pairs, encouraging the values of compromise, shared responsibility, and teamwork, so lacking in these difficult times. She gazed in a pained sort of a way out the far window. Thus would a small public school in the Village, in its own little way, act as a beacon for the world. It took a few minutes for Donovan to recognize in this new directive the last-minute reprieve for which he had not even dared to hope. 'Me and you!' cried a child called Donna Ford, grabbing the hand of another child called Carla Woodbeck, who flushed happily and replied, 'Yeah, us two!' and in another moment the room was filled with similar cries, requested and answered, all around Donovan, like a series of doors shutting in his face. Reduced to trying to catch the eye of Walter Ulbricht he found even Walter Ulbricht avoiding him, apparently holding out for a better option.

'Part of my point,' said Miss Steinhardt, in a queer wobbly voice that silenced her class, 'is we don't always get to choose whom we work with.' Miss Steinhardt had spent yesterday at her grandparents' home in Brooklyn Heights, watching tanks cross the Suez Canal. 'Line up please as I call your names.'

The pairing was to be achieved alphabetically, as if a third of the class wasn't coloured and Walter Ulbricht didn't have a port-wine stain eating half his face. A second flurry of anxious voices went up; Miss Steinhardt ignored them; the double line was achieved; the bell rang. In the hall, Cassandra Kent fell in step with Donovan Kendal. They walked out like this, onto Sullivan, neither holding hands nor talking, yet clearly walking together. Once again he passed through Washington Square Park, as he did daily, but the fact of Cassie Kent transformed it: the leaves were not merely crunchy but entirely golden, and the fountain threw up glorious columns of water, over and over, an engine of joy. Whatever it was that glistened in the wide skull-gaps between her tight plaits smelled of a vacation somewhere wonderful.

'Let's do yours,' said Cassie. 'The museum. Since you got it all figured already.'

'Oh. Well, all right.'

'Gu– gu– guggenheim,' she said, imitating him but somehow not unkindly. 'Now, it's gonna look like an ice cream, we know that.'

'A temple for the s— s— pirit. Hundred and ten feet tall,' said the boy, as they went under the arch. 'And this is, how tall d'you think —'

'Seventy-seven. So thirty per cent smaller,' said Cassie, without pausing. 'I'm mathematical. Wanna play?'

They took a left and sat on two stone benches under the shade of a sycamore tree, in front of a game Donovan had never before played in his life. Cassie drew a ratty string bag from her satchel and emptied a small pile of chess pieces onto the concrete table. Donovan tried to concentrate on her instructions. All around them, the men the Kendals usually took the long route round the park to avoid gathered close. One of them was completely topless under his shearling jacket and had old newspapers wound tightly round both shoes. Another had only a handful of teeth and wore a broken gambler's visor to keep the winter sun out of his eyes. He appeared to know Cassie.

'Hey, boy — you ready?' asked the visor man, of Donovan. He knelt down by both children and planted his rusty elbows on the table. 'This girl 'bout to school you.'

Donovan's plan was to watch each of Cassie's moves intently, hoping to follow the logic of the game, and, from there, recreate this logic in his own woolly mind. But where she moved her pieces ruthlessly over the concrete table, with an eye only to their strategic use, to Donovan these were noble Kings and Queens, and those were the castles in which they lived; here were the advisors they trusted, and there the minions waiting in lines outside the castle wall — and no amount of explanation from Cassie about the rigid rules that were meant to dictate all their movements could stop the boy from instinctively arranging his pieces by rank or relationship.

'Can't win anything, playing like that,' said Cassie, abducting Donovan's Queen, who had rashly stepped out of her chamber to stroke a favoured white steed. 'Can't even get *started* playing like that.'

By the time she had his King surrounded, not too long after they'd begun, she was sat up on her own heels, laughing and clapping her hands.

'Donovan Kendal,' she crowed, jabbing a finger into his sternum, 'you got no place to turn.'

'But couldn't this Cassie whoever-she-is just learn the lines?' Polly wanted to know. She was holding a tube of glue unwisely between her teeth. Her son passed the paper doily of Grandmother's cap and the cardboard face of the wolf, to be affixed to each other, a task that had to be redone almost every week. 'I mean, we could certainly do with another pair of hands.'

'But turns out it's got to be just two kids together. Just me and her. Teacher said so.'

'Well, all right, but I still don't see why that should –'

'She's a coloured girl,' said Donovan, hardly knowing why, but in its way, the intervention worked; for reasons of consistency it was now impossible for Polly to speak ill of the project. Anyone who knew anything at all about Polly Kendal knew she held the idea of Racial Integration almost as close to her heart as she did The Power of Storytelling or The Innocence of Children. Once upon a time – on what was back then a rare trip downtown – she herself had been caught up in the drama of Racial Integration, in the form of a large, excitable crowd pushing through Washington Square towards Judson Church. Being, by temperament, 'a lifelong seeker', she'd joined this crowd, finding herself, a few minutes later, three pews back from the podium listening to the young Reverend Martin Luther King Jr. give a speech. A lively story for coffee mornings and parent–teacher conferences. 'His eyes! The only word I can find for them is "limpid". Limpid. I could see them looking straight at me: this kooky, sixteen-year-old scrap of a white girl from Brighton Beach. I mean, naturally I stood out. And I'll tell you something else and I'm not the least bit ashamed of it: whatever he would have asked me to do, I would have done it! I would have done anything!' But as it happened the Reverend King had not asked the teenage Polly to do anything at all and her practical involvement with the civil rights movement ended with that sermon, leaving behind only a residuum of enthusiasm.

'Why *shouldn't* the children of Harlem get the equal chance to hear our stories?' she asked Cassie two days later, as the child pulled a rattan chair to a circular table covered by a fringed, gypsy cloth, missing only a crystal ball. 'Telling someone a story is a way of showing love. Don't they deserve love?'

'I love everybody!' said Cassie, happily, and accepted the breadstick that was passed to her. 'But: if I am attacked, I will defend. You play chess, Mr Kendal?'

'Me?' Irving lowered his newspaper. 'Nope. Not my game.'

'I play.'

'You do?' Polly stopped stirring her spaghetti sauce and took a second, anthropological look at Cassie Kent. There were the girls in pigtails who skipped and sang by the fountain, and then there were the grubby old men hunched over the stone tables by the far west gate, but the two groups had always been quite separate in her mind. 'At school, you mean?'

'In the park sometimes. Whenever, wherever. I'm pretty good, too.'

'I'll bet you are!'

'I beat Donovan good.'

'Cassie, do you know Donny *never* brings any of his friends round to see his poor Maw and Paw,' said Polly, putting her hands on slender hips and delving into her small trove of accents. 'So I'm real glad he thought to bring you round to see us.'

'I was gonna show-and-tell my chess . . . but when you think about it, there ain't that much to show.'

'Of course, *our* show is up and ready to go, any time,' said Polly, slowly. The train was coming back down the line, and Donovan, tied to the track, did his best to divert it.

'But that's not – you can't teach a person to do that in just a few days. Puppets are a real craft,' he said, quoting Polly back to Polly, which seemed to calm her; she stopped biting the spoon and put it back in the pot.

'Well, that's very true. It *is* a craft. Not everyone can pick it up just like that.'

'There's a war on,' said Irving loudly, and flicked a finger at the front page. 'Somebody should show-and-tell about that.'

Cassie examined the photograph: 'They your people over there?'

'Hmm?' said Polly, with her back to them all. 'Oh, no, not mine. Irving's. Technically. I mean, he doesn't have any relatives over there or anything.'

'*Technically?*'

The door caught on the usual tile and failed to slam; Polly did not flinch. Polly, Cassie and Donovan listened to Irving leave the cottage, and – such was the silence of the mews in those days – strike a match against an outside wall. Polly returned placidly to her sauce.

'Of course, in the end,' she said, with a contented look on her face, 'we're all one people.'

'This is a scale model,' said Cassie, holding up, in front of the class, a circular, inverted ziggurat made of cardboard, and Donovan read the scale off a piece of paper, and then Cassie said the name of the architect, and Donovan somehow got through the phrase 'gun-placed concrete' and it all passed off without a hitch. But in the hallway, afterwards, when they should have been simply congratulating each other, Cassie announced her intention to soon visit the Polly Kendal Puppet Theater.

'But – it's two bucks.'

'I'm not in the poorhouse – we got two bucks!'

'It's just for little kids,' tried Donovan, gripped by the horrible confirmation of a private fear – that all roads led back to his mother. 'You're too old. And it's on a S– s– sunday. You'll go to church, won't you?'

'I'm *coming*.'

'It's not two bucks, that was a lie,' said Donovan, turning red. Having put his hand up inside Pinocchio every Saturday for the whole of the previous year, he had been unable to rid himself of a feeling of deep identification. 'If you really want to know it's only fifty c– fifty c–'

Most adults would keep looking into his face when he was in trouble, smiling kindly, until the word, whatever it happened to be, was completed. Cassie, like all children, only said, 'What? *What? What?*' and groaned with impatience. She walked ahead. When he caught her up, she turned on him: 'Man oh man, can't you *stop* that?'

'Yes,' said Donovan, feebly, but perhaps that was just another lie. A man called Cory Wallace had assured the Kendals that their son could be easily 'cured' of his trouble, but he did not seem to be a proper doctor – he had no certificates on his wall and his office was next to a Chinese restaurant down on Canal. Still Polly had 'faith in his sincerity'.

'Donovan Kendal,' said Cassie, sighing and putting her hands on her hips like somebody's mother, 'you tire me out. Wanna see my titty?'

They were within spitting distance of their classroom; it did not seem a viable prospect. But in the turn of the stairwell, Cassie pressed herself against a wall and pulled her pinafore to one side. Donovan stared dumbly at a breast no different than his own except that the nipple was slightly larger and the skin a deep and lovely brown. He put his palm flat against its flatness. They stood there like that until a footstep was heard on the stair. 'If I was a hooker,' whispered Cassie, pulling the fabric back over and looking serious, 'that would be ten bucks easy.' After which they walked to the exit and parted without another word.

Matters developed. One morning before school, Donovan lunged at her and was rewarded with a long, chaste, beautiful kiss: two closed mouths pressed against each other while Cassie jerked her head violently back and forth, as perhaps she had seen people do in the movies. At an arbitrary moment, she pulled away and primly flattened her pinafore against her chest.

'Don't think I've forgotten,' she said. 'I'm coming to that show.' That same afternoon, in a restroom cubicle, he asked to see her 'ding-a-ling' and she obliged – a confusion of black folds that parted to reveal a shockingly pink interior. He was permitted to put one finger in and then take it out again. After which it was hard to see how he could refuse her.

Black folds, green velvet. Donovan peering through. He could see Cassie sitting with the adults on the chairs, her feet up by her bottom, hugging herself. 'Please remember,' said Polly backstage, drawing the heads of her crouching husband and son towards her own, 'I don't want to see Goldilocks *or* the bowls until I've dismantled the woodshed. You were much too quick with that, last week, both of you – but you, Irving, in particular.' Irving thrust his hand violently into Papa Bear: 'Don't tell me what to do. I know what I'm doing.' Donovan rang the little bell, and the churchwarden dimmed the 'house lights' and Goldilocks's hair got caught on a nail, and all this had happened before, many times. In a sort of dream, Donovan got off his knees and walked round the front to invite all the little believers to join him in the Land of Nod. He was sure enough that he said his lines (carefully written by Polly, free of the dangerous letters) and sang his song; he could hear the children yelling, and knew the brown smudge of the wolf must be behind him, appearing and disappearing, in rhythm with their cries. But all he could see was Cassie's upper lip pulled tight into her mouth, and the deep crease of her brow. Somehow, he got through the half-hour. The house lights went up. Polly was by his side once more, all in black, a tiny piece of punctuation, and she was saying My Husband Irving and My Son Donovan and they were all three holding hands and bowing.

'Cassie, you came!'

Polly reached both hands out to the girl. Cassie kept her own in the back pockets of her jeans.

'I'll tell you what: would you like to come backstage? There's a box of tricks back there.'

She led the girl behind the velvet to where Irving sat on the floor, smoking a cigarette, placing props and puppets into open shoeboxes. He held up the wolf and put it over Cassie's hand.

'You try – move it.'

Cassie moved it slightly to the right. Its Grandmother's cap came unglued and fell away. She handed it back to Irving.

'This god*damned* –'

Polly rescued the wolf from her husband before it could be flung, and placed it back with its cap softly in a box marked 'Bad Guys #2'.

'Why all the puppets so raggedy?' Cassie asked.

'Well . . . if they look home-made, I suppose that's because we make them ourselves.'

'Thought you meant puppets like puppets,' said Cassie, turning to Donovan. 'Like Howdy Doody or somebody.'

Polly stepped in: 'Well, that's really not a hand puppet. That's a marionette. Which is fine – if you like that sort of thing. But it's really not puppetry.'

'Puppets got arms and legs and bodies,' Cassie persisted, pointing to Goldilocks at rest. 'That's just a cut-out cardboard face. It ain't even got more than one side.'

Polly put an arm around Cassie and led her back out into the hall. 'I hope we see you again,' she said, speaking over Cassie's head to the fleeing families. 'We do a charity show in the Bronx, and in Harlem, once a month, paid for by your generous contributions. Do please leave what you can in the bottle by the door. We've been doing this show in this spot for almost six years! But not everyone's as fortunate as our children of Greenwich Village.' She put a hand on top of Cassie's head. 'It's a wonderful opportunity for the children up there.'

'I live on Tenth and Fourteenth,' protested Cassie, but Polly had moved on, and was now accosting her small audience as they tried to take their leave. And how did you come to hear of the Polly Kendal Puppet Theater? A friend? An advertisement? The unlucky few looked up rather desperately; more fortunate, dexterous women had already managed to wedge their children back into their coats and were halfway down Hudson by now. So which was it: 'Word-of-mouth' or 'Publicity'? It took a moment to understand that the latter category referred to those little four-by-six cards, poorly illustrated and printed, that were to be seen in practically every café, dive bar, jazz den and restaurant beneath Union Square.

'On the first of the month, we go to the November cycle: *The Musicians of Bremen*, *Goldilocks and the Three Bears*, and *Cinderella*. Tell your friends!' Across the hall, Donovan lingered, half-hidden by the stage curtain, trying to choose between a number of things to say. He was still preparing the sentence, checking it for what he thought of as 'snakes' and 'goblins', when Cassie Kent simply ran past him, into the church, down the aisle – and was gone.

The Kendals were alone. Shoeboxes were numbered, closed

and placed in a suitcase in their correct order. The three-sided 'stage' was flattened, and care taken to fold the green velvet into a clean square. Irving switched off all the lights and collected a handful of dollars from the jar. Polly sat lightly on the closed suitcase and pressed its brass clips down.

'What happened to your little friend?'

Donovan pulled the nightcap off his own head and held it in both hands.

'But Donny . . . why would you even want to spend your time with a girl like that? Oh, I'm sure she's nice enough – I don't want to put you off her if you really *like* her, but she seemed to me to be so clearly – well, she has so little, oh, I don't know: fancy. Imagination. Whimsy. Trust me: you don't want that. Irving has no imagination whatsoever and look how hard that makes just about everything. A sense of imagination is so much more important to me than what colour someone happens to be or how much money they have or anything like that – if *that's* what you think you're standing there frowning about. The only thing I care about is what's going on in here,' she said, and thumped her narrow chest, but Donovan only looked at his shoes.

'Listen to me. Why do you think she doesn't like you? Because you have a little trouble sometimes when you speak? Because you're skinny? Don't you see that if she had even a scrap of vision she'd see what a first-class kid you are? But she's got no vision to speak of. I bet she's going home right now to turn on that idiot box and just *vegetate*.' Now his mother performed a funny mime – eyes crossed, tongue tucked in front of lower teeth – and Donovan found it impossible not to smile.

'All she does is watch TV,' he confided, and let the cap drop to the stone floor where he worried it with his foot a little. 'All weekend. She told me one time. Her mom doesn't care what she does, she really doesn't care one bit,' he added, employing a little imagination, 'and they never read or anything. The whole family thinks reading's a big waste of time. She's never heard of Thor or the Sirens or anybody!'

'Well, there you are.'

Polly bent down, picked up Wee Willie Winkie's nightcap, and with great tenderness, brushed the dust off it and placed it back on her son's head.

'People find their natural level, Donny. You'll see when you're older. It all works out.'

Parents' Morning Epiphany

1. Welcome to the Narrative Techniques Worksheet!
2. Feel free to take this worksheet home and review it with your child.
3. Let's get going!

Narrative Writers Use Techniques Such As . . .

Dialogue

The illustration underneath, on the children's worksheet, is a blank speech bubble. Nothing in it – just empty space. And yet in this matter, the worksheet is surely correct: these days it's best to say nothing.

Revealing Actions

Here we have three sets of stick figures, all with big bellies. They are racially ambivalent (although one stick figure in each set has curly hair). Nobody has genitals, but one figure in each pairing has long hair, so come to your own conclusions. In the first set, let's say that the male – the one with short curly hair – is pushing over the long-haired girl. Stick figures are not by their nature expressive but she looks traumatized. In the second illustration, she has given her attacker a balloon. It's not clear why. Maybe to apologize for being the victim? They're both smiling. In the third iteration, they're hugging. Much has been revealed, but much remains unspoken.

Multiple Points of View

A girl looks through a magnifying glass. Next to her, a boy looks through a magnifying glass. Next to him, a cat looks through a magnifying glass. This apparently exhausts the question of perspective.

1st Person Narrator

A boy looking mightily pleased with himself holds a pencil bigger than his own head. Out of his actual head come three separate speech bubbles: 'I' and 'ME' and 'MY'. Well, *exactly.*

Inner Thinking

Very curious. It's the blank speech bubble again but this time, instead of its own emptiness being described by a nice smooth line, now the line is crinkled and fluffy, like a cloud. Is what we think somehow more crinkly and fluffy than what we dare to say out loud? Or more dreamlike? Or more empty? The worksheet, intended, as it is, for fourth graders, avoids these secondary questions.

Description

A painting rests upon an easel. A paintbrush is suspended in air, near the easel, but not in anybody's hand. The picture itself is a realistic pastoral scene: a little house, with smoke coming from the chimney, a field, a tree, the moon. Is the worksheet implying that description can and should only concern itself with the visible? That the work of description is to re-inscribe the real? That the real, as it is conceived by the artist, should be by definition picturesque or pastoral? What kind of a work-sheet is this?

Use Transitions

A clock shows the time. It is a featureless clock with only hands, no numbers, but the time looks to be about ten past four. (I do not believe there is a hidden meaning in this.) Around the clock are some helpful suggestions: *A little later. Later. After that. The following day. Next!*

Turn Over the Worksheet

Okay.

Narrative Writers Aim Towards Goals Such As . . .

Set Up the Problem

A car is speeding towards a cliff edge. The cliff edge is icy, it is midwinter. There is also a random tree branch sticking out halfway down the side of the icy cliff. An exclamation mark is written into the sky itself. You have to hand it to the worksheet: that's a hell of a set-up.

Introduce the Characters

Small stick kid with what looks like Bantu knots and glasses. Tall stick woman with Lana Del Rey haircut. Tiny baby stick figure, crying, with single curl springing from head. Old stick figure with grandmotherly hair tied in a bun, walking with a cane. Arrows point to all of them, as if to say, LOOK AT ALL THESE CHARACTERS. But perhaps there are other ways to do this, beyond the worksheet's ken.

Show the Character's Motivation

The Bantu-headed kid, glasses gone, is holding a gift-wrapped present. In his innermost thoughts – represented within a cloud-like bubble – he is dreaming of giving his gift to the girl with the Lana Del Rey haircut. And this, the classic love story, is indeed the motivation for many a narrative writer and yet how can I confess to the worksheet that it has never interested me in the least?

Stir Empathy

Stir empathy! Here is a bowl, on which is written EMPATHY. The bowl appears to be filled with a thick, dark, swirly liquid, like melted chocolate. It is stirred by a spoon with a heart on it. Stir empathy! An aesthetic principle or an ethical one – or both? Hard to say. But on the main point there can be no argument: to stir empathy is the aim and purpose of all stories, everywhere, always. How can you doubt it? It's written right there in black and white on the worksheet!

Create the Setting

The easel is back, with the same painting, and the suspended brush. The New York Public School Board turns out to be a very insistent proponent of literary Realism.

Show the Resolution

The car is gone, the man is out of the car, and he's standing on the edge of the ice-covered cliff, clearly relieved, stick hand to his stick head, just saying PHEW. Don't ask me how that happened. Plot is not my strong point.

Draw in Your Reader

A recognizable human boy with sneakers and hair and actual legs lies on his belly upon the floor, reading delightedly from a book, lost in it completely. Oh, I remember that feeling!

Clarity of Ideas

A magnifying glass. Just that. No one's holding it and nothing's being magnified. It's like some kind of Zen *kōan*. It may have gone over my head.

I Made Revisions with my Goals in Mind

It's a notepad being worked over by a pencil but the absence of a human figure suggests to me that the worksheet knows full well (but daren't tell the children) that the goal never truly comes before the revision but is created precisely by the revision itself.

The Theme is Woven Through the Story

It's the same notepad, but now the pencil is a needle and thread and the word it's sewing into the pad is: *theme*. I can imagine, a hundred years from now, this worksheet being found in the flooded wreckage of what was once New York, and a small religious sect forming around its precepts, and this penultimate instruction being the holiest tenet of their faith.

Clearly Move Through Time

A boy is running. Behind him it says SPEED THINGS UP. A turtle passes him, heading in the opposite direction. Behind her it says SLOW THINGS DOWN. Well, that's the whole trick of the thing, right there.

Downtown

A great Austrian painter – he lives in a forest in Hungary – came by the apartment one day, with his daughters, both red-headed with pigtails, pale-faced, silent. They wore the kind of clothes you can't buy in any shop, you have to get them delivered direct from the turn of the century. Fucking angels, both of them. Meanwhile my kids raged around the place, dressed as tiny long-distance truckers, hyped-up on sour gummies. They clung to their tablets as if to items necessary for their very survival – colostomy bags, say. But I refused to be ashamed. Like everyone else in America these days I stand in my truth.

On the other hand, he *is* a terrific painter. Of all the living painters he is the most livingiest and also the most painterly. About four years ago he found a whole new vernacular to the point that nobody sees much point in painting any more, and so he has somehow both revivified painting and killed it off simultaneously. Of course, we're all terribly jealous. His occasional visits to the city mean an awful lot and I was honoured this time to get to be the one to host him and his pair of silent angels. I'd invited a few of my downtown crowd to touch the hem of his garment, but when he walked in with his girls we all saw straight away that there would be no garment-touching and no way would he agree to come to Café Loup with us to chew on some tough schnitzel and get blasted till the early hours. He's the real deal, and therefore, like his daughters, mostly silent. Honestly, it was how I imagine it might be to have Schopenhauer round to tea. An honour and a privilege, sure, but socially pretty hard work. He stayed about an hour and a half. Said maybe two paragraphs of human words, none of which turned out to be metaphysical or existential or even aesthetic. How to get to x or y on the L, at which hotel he was staying, when and where the children might eat. Long silences in between. Finally, it was time to go. At the doorway he said, as if it had just occurred to him: 'I don't understand how you can live here, and be an artist, amongst all this social noise and all of these people. I myself live in an Hungarian forest.' It was the kind of statement calculated to drive me into a frenzy of self-hatred. I thanked him for his enquiry – and his 'an' – and pointed him in the direction of the L. Then I sent everyone home and got in a funk for a few days.

The New York Public School Calendar does not recognize funks, personal, existential, artistic or otherwise. School starts on September 4th and that's that. The only way to get out of it is to take an ordinary belt, tie it round your neck, loop it round a door handle and then sit suddenly upon the floor. Although this method likely won't get your kid out of having to turn up on that first day, it will at least mean you don't have to take them. It was September 4th – I had to take them. In the line to get through the school gates – a momentous line, which snakes from Café Loup all the way down Sixth Avenue like a tapeworm of the Devil – a parent started talking to me about his family's transformative summer break to the jungles of Papua

New Guinea. It had taken three planes to get there, they'd gone to bed with monkeys and woken up with sloths and the whole trip had been utterly transformative: transformative to escape the American 'situation', transformative for him personally, and for his wife, and for the children, but especially for him. Transformative. I peered at this dude very closely. I hadn't seen him since last September 4th but to my painterly eye he didn't appear especially transformed. Seemed like much the same asshole.

On the sad, childless walk home, I heard a very old white lady outside Citarella exclaim loudly, into her phone: 'But he's not my friend, he's my *driver*!' To which a tall boy in sequinned culottes with a Basquiat 'fro – who happened to be passing – replied: 'Lady, you are GOALS.' My concern about both jungles and forests is that you can't really imagine anything like that happening in them.

I was in such a funk I left town for a few days, taking a train down the Eastern Seaboard. I read E. M. Cioran and agreed with him when he said he agreed with Josep Pla who had previously agreed with himself that we are nothing but it's hard to admit it. In the Potomac, at seven in the morning, I saw four men in a little canoe, all facing forward, with a heroic cast to their faces. You'd have thought they were bringing a body back from a fatal duel. I watched as their craft moved silently through the water and the fog, past the Washington Monument. At the bow, a single pilot light. It was all so beautiful. It was a symbol of something. I considered looking into local forest real estate. But I missed the city.

By the time I got back (I'd spent longer away than I'd thought) Café Loup had closed, Dr Ford was testifying, and the combination of these events was causing mass hysteria below 14th Street. The café had actually closed in the summer, the very same day somebody (the city?) had installed a large yellow megaphone at the crossroads of Greenwich and Sixth, at which megaphone what happens is, when you press the button beside whatever historic Greenwich Village writer's name is by that particular button, well, what happens is you hear them reading a few lines of their writing, thus affirming the past cultural significance of the village despite all present evidence to the contrary. You can press Willa Cather you can press Amiri Baraka you can press Frank O'Hara you can press Jimmy Baldwin I could go on. But because of the culturally insensitive timing what was actually happening as we walked by was a crazy young man with a fashion haircut was running up to the megaphone at intervals and screaming *into* it: CAFÉ LOUP HAS CLOSED! CAFÉ LOUP HAS CLOSED! Me and my kids sat down on the bright red wrought-iron furniture the city has set up at that traffic circle and watched him go. CAFÉ LOUP HAS CLOSED! Then he'd run down the street and you'd think that was the end of it but a minute later he'd be back, tight white jeans all sweaty, fashion hair whipping around in the breeze, still screaming: CAFÉ LOUP HAS CLOSED! THIS IS NOT A DRILL! CAFÉ LOUP HAS CLOSED! My son asked me if the young man was 'sick in the head' which is our downtown euphemism for batshit crazy, but my daughter who is very, very savvy said, 'No way – look at his clothes!' I thought that was an interesting answer. It meant she was becoming an American. It meant she now refused to believe rich people can be batshit crazy.

On Sunday, I went to Black Church to worship Monie Love and Dead Prez (featuring Jay). The minister led us through the catechism:

Monie in the middle

Where she at?

In the middle

Amen to that! Then we moved on to the body of the sermon, which was on our daily struggle:

You don't like that do ya?

You fucked up the hood?

Nigga, right back to you!

Hell yeah!

You know we tired of starving my nigga!

And lo, I was in awe. To heareth the mode in which Dead Prez doth breaketh it down, economically. Seeingeth the whole game from top to bottom. Maybe there is no such game in an Hungarian forest, but I don't live in an Hungarian forest, I live right here, and I was listening to the stone cold truth. I was deeply moved. We came together in prayer. We prayed for:

Sandra Bland

Trayvon Martin

Eric Garner

Alton Sterling

Philando Castile

Michael Brown

We did not stop there but I am practising an economy of form. And the minister took us all in his embrace, in a human chain, and he did say: Now we shall come together in prayer for this young child who was shot because she was black. And God help me but I broke the chain. I said, See what you've done there is you've transformed an act of the perpetrator into a characteristic of the target. You've turned one person's action into another person's being. I said, You don't say to a witch: *the reason they're dunking you is because you're a witch.* You say, the reason they're dunking you is these motherfuckers believe in witchcraft! Their whole society is based on it! Nobody put a spell on them! They produce witchcraft every day, collectively, together! Their whole reality is constructed on a belief in witchcraft!

Well, Black Church got what I was saying but it wasn't anything they hadn't heard before and plus they didn't feel it was particularly helpful in the present moment what with witches getting dunked right, left and centre, every fucking place you looked. The minister took me aside and said: Now, you're not American, are you? So you're kind of talking out your ass, if you'll excuse my technical religious language. And I said, Minister, you're absolutely right, I am from the Caribbean side of things, and, like the pesky Africans, we haven't yet learned the catechism fully. It takes years and years of training to fully concede you are a witch. But I'm amenable! I can be taught!

Two of my aunts came to town, just in time for Brett to make his case. Being Jamaican ladies of a certain dimension we took up a lot of the sidewalk and enjoyed ourselves thoroughly. We started walking in Harlem and headed downtown, but my aunts still have the habit of making a little note in a calfskin notebook every time they see a glorious individual from the diaspora and by the time we got to Greene Street they'd seen seven hundred painters, three hundred and seventy-nine video and conceptual artists, about eight hundred writers, an infinity amount of musicians, forty-seven sculptors in various materials, a whole load of doctors and entertainment lawyers, plenty yoga teachers and so on and whatnot, plus a former President, Lyle Ashton Harris, John Legend, Hilton Als and Spike Lee himself. I said, Ladies, you're gonna wear out those notebooks, you might as well try and take it all in your stride. We haven't even got to Brooklyn! (Of course, I could have taken them elsewhere but they come from elsewhere and I wanted to show them the sparkling lights like any good niece on the tourist trail.) My aunts gave me the side eye. They folded their arms under their mighty bosoms. They said, Dear yellowbone niece, don't be hurrying us on our holidays – let us take our sweet time. Maybe we *were* made witches, but this beautiful, globe-stretching coven you're a part of is what we did with what was done to us, it is our own blessed creation, and a mighty glorious business it is too! Therefore: hush up. Let us enjoy it while we're here. Now do you know where Lorraine Hansberry's plaque is or do you not?

Anyway, by the time we got to the tip of the island they were in high racial spirits and didn't mind too much settling into a corner booth and watching the proceedings from Washington on a massive TV hung above the bar. Now, rape is as common in the history of our family as whatever is common in your family is common in yours, so what my aunts said next I take to have a certain authority. They said, This might look like a war between men and women, but what this really is is the last siege of a ruling class. See Brett up there making that little bitch-baby face? See that? That's the face a baby makes when you try and take his rattle away. We've had many, many babies so we're familiar. America being the rattle in this analogy. He thinks he deserves to do whatever he wants with that rattle, and women are simply a subclause in that arrangement. Remember when we pressed the button on that crazy yellow megaphone? When we heard blessed LeRoi Jones cry out THE NATION IS LIKE OURSELVES? But dear yellowbone niece as we have explained we are on holiday and we are here to have a good time. Can't we go dancing now?

We danced for four days, which turned out to be the exact length of the investigation, and by the time my aunts' taxi pulled in at JFK, Brett had proved once again that whenever a young Brett is born in these United States, born with a dream, that dream can truly come true. Yes, sir, if your baby Brett really puts his mind to it – if he believes, if he has faith, if he is a he, and if he is called Brett – he can do whatever it is he puts his mind to, and that goes double for all you Troys, Kips, Tripps, Bucks and Chads.

Well, we were reeling. And I'm not the conspiratorial type but it did seem a bit suspicious that just as Brett was getting sworn in, everybody beneath 14th Street got an email informing them that Café Loup was reopening. I think even a true artist living in an Hungarian forest can imagine that in the circumstances this felt like the best news any of us had heard in the longest time. I tried on four different outfits and then just went ahead and wore them all. I ran through the doors. It was packed to the rafters. But once you got over the incredible crush of human bodies it was impossible not to notice that not a thing had changed. The wallpaper was the same, the waiters were the same, the food was still not especially good, the tables were as usual flung randomly around the place, and everyone still thought the Austrian painter had either opened the door to a new possibility in painting or destroyed the possibility of painting altogether. The only difference was that instead of drinking our usual Martinis while discussing this infinite subject, everybody was drinking beer, and clinking beers, and telling their waiters as they served more beer: 'Sometimes I drank too much. Sometimes others did. I liked beer. I still like beer.' I suppose that kind of thing is why real artists live in Hungarian forests, but I live downtown so I took my seat at a series of different tables (the whole point of Café Loup is it's a movable feast) and told everyone I met that the next time they saw me in this godforsaken joint or Black Church or anywhere else for that matter I'd have shed my Green Card and become a citizen because really what the fuck and the great thing about Café Loup is nobody rolled their eyes or pointed out the delicate matter of a new citizen's eligibility for certain national art prizes until I was way down Sixth Avenue and couldn't hear a thing.

Miss Adele Amidst the Corsets

'Well, that's that,' Miss Dee Pendency said, and Miss Adele, looking back over her shoulder, saw that it was. The strip of hooks had separated entirely from the rest of the corset. Dee held up the two halves, her big red slash mouth pulling in opposite directions.

'Least you can say it died in battle. Doing its duty.'

'Bitch, I'm on in ten minutes.'

'When an irresistible force like your ass . . .'

'Don't sing.'

'Meets an old immovable object, like this shitty old corset . . . You can bet as sure as you liiiiive!'

'It's your fault. You pulled too hard.'

'Something's gotta give, something's gotta give, SOMETHING'S GOTTA GIVE.'

'You pulled too hard.'

'Pulling's not your problem.' Dee lifted her bony white Midwestern leg up onto the counter, in preparation to put on a thigh-high. With a heel she indicated Miss Adele's mountainous box of chicken and rice: 'Real talk, baby.'

Miss Adele sat down on a grubby velvet stool and greeted her reflection. She was thickening and sagging, in all the same ways, in all the same places, as her father. Plus it was midwinter, her skin was ashy. She felt like some once-valuable piece of mahogany furniture, lightly dusted with cocaine. This final battle with her corset had set her wig askew. She was forty-six years old.

'Lend me yours.'

'Good idea. You can wear it on your arm.'

And tired to death, as the Italians say – tired to *death*. Especially sick of these kids, these 'Millennials', or whatever they were calling themselves. Always 'on'. No backstage to any of them – only front of house. Wouldn't know a sincere, sisterly friendship if it kicked down the dressing-room door and sat on their faces.

Miss Adele stood up, un-taped, put a furry deerstalker on her head and switched to her comfortable shoes. She removed her cape. Maybe stop with the cape? She had only to catch herself in the mirror at a bad angle, and there was Daddy, in his robes.

'The thing about undergarments,' Dee said, 'is they can only do so much with the cards they've been dealt? Like Obama.'

'Stop talking.'

Miss Adele zipped herself into a cumbersome floor-length padded coat, tested – so the label claimed – by climate scientists in the Arctic.

'Looking swell, Miss Adele.'

'Am I trying to impress somebody? Only thing waiting for me at the stage door is mono. Tell Jake I went home.'

'He's out front – tell him yourself!'

'I'm heading this way.'

'You know what they say about choosing between your ass and your face?'

Miss Adele put her shoulder to the fire door and heaved it open. She caught the punchline in the ice-cold stairwell.

'You should definitely choose one of those at some point.'

Aside from having to work there, Miss Adele tried not to mess much with the East Side. She'd had the same sunny rent-controlled studio apartment on Tenth Avenue and 23rd since '93, and loved the way the West Side communicated with the water and the light, loved the fancy galleries and the big anonymous condos, the High Line funded by bankers and celebrities, the sensation of clarity and wealth.

But down here? Depressing. Even worse in the daylight. Crappy old buildings higgledy-piggledy on top of each other, ugly students, shitty pizza joints, delis, tattoo parlours. Nothing bored Miss Adele more than ancient queens waxing lyrical about the good old bad old days. At least the bankers never tried to rape you at knife-point or sold you bad acid. And then once you got past the Village, everything stopped making sense. Fuck these little streets with their dumbass names! And then the logistics of googling one's location – remove gloves, put on glasses, find the damn phone – were too much to contemplate in the current wind chill. Instead Miss Adele stalked violently up and down Rivington, cutting her eyes at any soul who dared look up. At the kerb she stepped over a frigid pool of yellow fluid, three cardboard plates frozen within it. What a dump! Let the city pull down everything under East 6th, rebuild, number it, make it logical, pack in the fancy hotels – not just one or two but a whole bunch of them. Don't *half*-gentrify – follow through. Stop preserving all this old shit.

Miss Adele had a right to her opinions. Thirty years in a city gives you the right. And now that she was, at long last, no longer beautiful, her opinions were all she had. They were all she had left to give to people.

Whenever her disappointing twin brother, Devin, deigned to call her from his three-kids-and-a-labradoodle, don't-panic-it's-organic, liberal-negro-wet-dream-of-a-Marin-County fantasy existence, Miss Adele made a point of gathering up all her hard-won opinions and giving them to him good. 'I wish he could've been mayor for ever. FOR-EVAH. I wish he was my boyfriend. I wish he was my *daddy*.' Or: 'They should frack the hell out of this whole state. We'll get rich, secede from the rest of you dope-smoking, debt-ridden assholes. You the ones dragging us all down.' Her brother accused Miss Adele of turning rightwards in old age. It would be more accurate to say that she was done with all forms of drama – politics included. That's what she liked about gentrification, in fact: gets rid of all the drama.

And who was left, anyway, to get dramatic about? Every pretty boy she'd ever cared about had already moved to Brooklyn, Jersey, Fire Island, Provincetown, San Francisco or the grave. This simplified matters. Work, pay cheque, apartment, the various lifestyle sections of *The Times*, Turner Classic Movies, Nancy Grace, bed. Boom. Maybe an old *Golden Girls* re-run. A little *Downton*. That was her routine and disruptions to it – like having to haul ass across town during a polar vortex to buy a new corset – were rare. Sweet Jesus, this cold! Unable to feel her toes, she stopped a shivering young couple in the street. British tourists, as it turned out; clueless, nudging each other and beaming up at her Adam's apple with delight, like she was in their guidebook, right next to the Magnolia Bakery and the Naked Cowboy. They had a map, but without her glasses it was useless. They had no idea where they were. 'Sorry! Stay warm!' they cried, and hurried off, giggling into their North Face jackets. Miss Adele tried to remember that her new thing was that she positively liked all the tourists and missed Bloomberg and loved Midtown and the Central Park nags and all the Prada stores and *The Lion King* and lining up for cupcakes wherever they happened to be located. Sure, why not, she was crazy about all that shit. So give those British kids your most winning smile. Sashay round the corner in your fur-cuffed Chelsea boots with the discreet heel. Once out of sight, though, it all fell apart; the smile, the straightness of her spine, everything. Even if you don't mess with it – even when it's not seven below – it's a tough city. Takes a certain wilfulness to keep your shit in a straight line. When did the effort start outweighing the pleasure? Part of the pleasure used to be precisely this: the buying of things. She used to *love* buying things! Lived for it! Now if she never bought another damn thing again she wouldn't even –

Clinton Corset Emporium. No awning, just a piece of cardboard stuck in the window. As Miss Adele entered, a bell tinkled overhead – an actual bell, on a catch wire – and she found herself in a long narrow room – a hallway really – with a counter down the left-hand side and a curtained-off cubicle at the far end, for privacy. Clearly it lacked many of the things a girl expects from an emporium – background music, hangers, shelves, mirrors, lights, price tags, et cetera. Bras and corsets were everywhere, piled on top of each other in anonymous white cardboard boxes, towering up to the ceiling. They seemed to form the very walls of the place.

'Good afternoon,' said Miss Adele, daintily removing her gloves, finger by finger. ' I am looking for a corset. Could somebody help me?'

A radio was on; talk radio — incredibly loud. Some AM channel bringing the latest from a distant land, where the people talk from the back of their throats. One of those Easterny, Russiany places? Miss Adele was no linguist, and no geographer. She unzipped her coat, made a noise in the back of her own throat, and looked pointedly at the presumed owner of the place. He sat slumped behind the counter, listening to this radio with a tragic twist to his face, like one of those sad-sack cab drivers you see hunched over the wheel, permanently tuned in to the bad news from back home. And what the point of *that* was, Miss Adele would never understand. Turn that shit down! Keep your eyes on the road! Leave the place you left where you left it! Lord knows, the day Miss Adele stepped out of the godforsaken state of Florida was pretty much the last day that shithole ever crossed her mind.

Could he even see her? He was angled away, his head resting in one hand. Looked to be about Miss Adele's age, but further gone: bloated face, about sixty pounds overweight, bearded, religious type, wholly absorbed by the radio. Meanwhile, somewhere back there, behind the curtain, Miss Adele could make out two women talking:

'She just turned fourteen. Why you don't speak to the nice lady? She's trying to help you. She just turned fourteen.'

'So she's still growing. We gotta consider that. Wendy – can you grab me a Brava 32 B?'

A scrap of an Asian girl appeared from behind the curtain, proceeded straight to the counter and vanished below it.

Miss Adele turned back to the owner. He had his fists stacked like hot potatoes – upon which he rested his chin – and his head tilted in apparent appreciation of what Miss Adele would later describe as 'the ranting', for did it not penetrate every corner of that space? And was it not quite impossible to ignore? She felt she had not so much entered a shop as some stranger's spittle-filled mouth. RAGE AND RIGHTEOUSNESS, cried this radio – in whatever words it used – RIGHTEOUSNESS AND RAGE. Miss Adele crossed her arms in front of her chest, like a shield. Not this voice – not today. Not any day – not for Miss Adele. By the time she'd hit New York, thirty years earlier, she already knew how to avoid being turned into a pillar of salt, and was not in the least bit surprised to find herself spending forty days – or four years – in the wilderness (of Avenue A). And though she had learned, over two decades, that there was nowhere on earth entirely safe from the voices of rage and righteousness – not even the new New York – still Miss Adele had taken great care to organize her life in such a way that her encounters with them were as few as possible. (On Sundays, she did her groceries in a cut-off T-shirt that read THOU SHALT.) She may have been fully immersed, dunked in the local water, with her daddy's hand on the back of her head and his blessing in her ear, but she'd leapt out of that shallow channel of water the first moment she was able. Was she to be ambushed, now, in a corset emporium?

'A corset,' she repeated, and raised her spectacular eyebrows. 'Could do with a little help here?'

'WENDY,' yelled the voice behind the curtain, 'could you see to our customer?'

The shop girl sprung puppet-like, up from below, clutching a stepladder to her chest.

'Looking for Brava!' shouted the girl, turned her back on Miss Adele, opened the stepladder and began to climb it. Meanwhile, the owner shouted something at the woman behind the curtain, and the woman, adopting his tongue, shouted something back. The radio voice worked itself up into what sounded like apoplexy.

'It is customary, in retail –' Miss Adele began.

'Sorry – one minute,' said the girl, came down with a box under her arm, dashed right past Miss Adele and disappeared once more behind the curtain.

Miss Adele took a deep breath. She stepped back from the counter, pulled her deerstalker off her head and tucked a purple bang behind her ear. Sweat prickled her face for the first time in weeks. She was considering turning on her heel and making that little bell shake till it fell off its damn string when the curtain opened and a mousy girl emerged, with her mother's arm around her. They were neither of them great beauties. The girl had a pissy look on her face, and moved with an angry slouch, like a prisoner, whereas you could see the mother was at least doing her best to keep things on an even keel. The mother looked beat – and too young to have a teenager. Or maybe she was the exact right age. Devin's kids were teenagers now. And Miss Adele was almost as old as the President. None of it made any sense, and yet you were still expected to accept it, and carry on, as if it were the most natural process in the world.

'Because they're not like hands and feet,' a warm and lively voice explained, behind the curtain, 'they grow independently.'

'Thank you so much for your advice, Mrs Alexander,' said

the mother, the way you talk to a priest through a screen. 'The trouble is this thickness here. All the women in our family got it, unfortunately. Curved ribcage.'

'But actually, you know – it's inneresting – it's a totally different curve from you to her. Did you realize that?'

The curtain opened. The speaker was revealed to be a lanky, wasp-waisted woman in her early fifties, with a long, humane face – dimpled, self-amused – and an impressive mass of thick chestnut hair.

'Two birds, two stones. That's the way we do it here. Everybody needs something different. That's what the big stores won't do for you. Individual attention. Mrs Berman, can I give you a tip?' The young mother looked up at the long-necked Mrs Alexander, a duck admiring a swan. 'Keep it on all the time. Listen to me, I know of what I speak. I'm wearing mine right now, I wear it every day. In my day they gave it to you when you walked out the hospital!'

'Well, you look amazing.'

'Smoke and mirrors. Now, all *you* need is to make sure the straps are fixed right like I showed you.' She turned to the sulky daughter and put a fingertip on each of the child's misaligned shoulders. 'You're a lady now, a beautiful young lady, you –' But here again she was interrupted from behind the counter, a sharp exchange of brutal and mysterious phrases, in which – to Miss Adele's satisfaction – the wife appeared to get the final word. Mrs Alexander took a cleansing breath and continued: 'So you gotta hold yourself like a lady. Right?' She lifted the child's chin and placed her hand for a moment on her cheek. 'Right?' The child straightened up, despite herself. See, some people are trying to ease your passage through this world – so ran Miss Adele's opinion – while others just want to block you at every damn turn. Think of poor Mamma, cupping her hand around a table's sharp corner, to protect the skull of one of her passing toddlers. That kind of instinctive, unthinking care. Now that Miss Adele had grown into the clothes of a middle-aged woman, she began to notice this new feeling of affinity toward them, far deeper than she had ever felt for young women, back when she could still fit into the hot-pants of a showgirl. She walked through the city struck by these strange partnerships of the soft and the hard. In shops, in restaurants, in line at the CVS. She always had the same question. Why in God's name are you *still* married to this asshole? Lady, your children are grown. You have your own credit cards. You're the one with life force. Can't you see he's just a piece of the furniture? It's not 1850. This is New York. Run, baby, run!

'Who's waiting? How can I help you?'

Mother and daughter duck followed the shop girl to the counter, to settle up. The radio, after a brief pause, made its way afresh up the scale of outrage. And Miss Adele? Miss Adele turned like a flower to the sun.

'Well, I need a new corset. A strong one.'

Mrs Alexander beamed: 'Come right this way.'

Together, they stepped into the changing area. But as Miss Adele reached to pull the curtain closed behind them both – separating the ladies from the assholes – a look passed between wife and husband and Mrs Alexander caught the shabby red velvet swathe in her hand, a little higher up than Miss Adele had, and held it open.

'Wait – let me get Wendy in here. I actually have to go speak with my husband about something. You'll be all right? The curtain's for modesty. You modest?'

She had a way about her. Her face expressed emotion in layers: elevated, ironic eyebrows, mournful violet eyes and sly, elastic mouth. She looked like one of the old movie stars. But which one?

'You're a funny lady,' said Miss Adele.

'A life like mine, you have to laugh – Marcus, *please*, one minute –' For he was barking at her – really going for it – practically insisting that she *stop talking to that schwarʒe*, which prompted Mrs Alexander to lean out of the changing room to say something like: *What is wrong with you? Can't you see I'm busy here?* before turning back with a strained smile to her new friend and confidante, Miss Adele. 'Is it okay if I don't measure you personally? Wendy can do it in a moment. I've just got to deal with – but listen, if you're in a hurry, don't panic, our eyes, they're like hands.'

'Can I just show you what I had?'

'Please.'

Miss Adele unzipped her handbag and pulled out the ruin.

'Oh! You're breaking my heart! From here?'

'I don't remember. It's possible. But maybe ten years ago.'

'Makes sense, we don't sell these any more. Ten years is ten years. Time for a change. What's it to go under? Strapless? Short? Long?'

'Everything. I'm trying to hide some of this.'

'You and the rest of the world. Well, that's my job.' She leaned over and put her lips just a little shy of Miss Adele's ear: 'Now I'm going to whisper. What you got up there? You can tell me. Flesh or feathers?'

'Not the former.'

'Got it. WENDY! I need a Futura and a Queen Bee, corsets, front fastening, forty-six. Bring a forty-eight, too. Marcus – please. One minute, okay? And bring the Paramount in, too! The crossover! Some people, you ask them these questions, they get offended. Everything offends them. Personally, I don't believe in "political correctness",' she said, articulating the phrase carefully, with great sincerity, as if she had recently coined it. 'My mouth's too big. I gotta say what's on my mind! Now, when Wendy comes, take off everything to here and try each corset on at its tightest setting. If you want a defined middle, frankly it's going to hurt. But I'm guessing you know that already.'

'Loretta Young,' called Miss Adele to Mrs Alexander's back, as she approached the counter. 'You look like Loretta Young. Know who that is?'

'Do I know who Loretta Young is? Excuse me one minute, will you?'

Mrs Alexander lifted her arms and said something to her husband, the only parts of which Miss Adele could fully comprehend were the triple repetition of the phrase 'Loretta Young'. In response, the husband made a noise somewhere between a sigh and a grunt.

'Do me a favour,' said Mrs Alexander, turning back to Miss Adele. 'Put it in writing, put it in the mail – then he can read it over and over. He's a reader.'

The curtain closed. But not entirely. An inch hung open and through it Miss Adele watched a silent movie – silent only in the sense that the gestures were everything. It was a marital drama, conducted in another language, but otherwise identical to those she and Devin had watched as children, through a crack in the door of their parents' bedroom. Appalled, fascinated, she watched the husband, making his noxious point, whatever it was (*You bring shame upon this family?*), and Mrs Alexander, apparently objecting (*I've given my life to this family?*); she watched as he became belligerent (*You should be ashamed?*) and she grew sarcastic (*Right, because you're such a good man?*), their voices competing with the radio (*THOU SHALT NOT?*), and reaching an unreasonable level of drama. Miss Adele strained to separate the sounds into words she might google later. If only there was an app that translated the arguments of strangers! A lot of people would buy that app. Miss Adele had read in *The Times* that a person could make eight hundred grand off such an app – just for having the *idea* for the app. (And Miss Adele had always considered herself a person of many ideas, really a very creative person who happened never to have quite found her medium; a person who, in more recent years, had often wondered whether finally the world and technology had caught up with precisely the kind of creative talents she had long possessed, although they had been serially and tragically neglected, first by her parents – who had wanted twin boy preachers – and later by her teachers, who saw her only as an isolated black child in Bible college, a sole Egyptian among the Israelites; and finally in New York, where her gifts had taken second place to her cheekbones and her ass.) You want to know what Miss Adele would do with eight hundred grand? She'd buy a studio down in Battery Park, and do nothing all day but watch the helicopters fly over the water. (And if you think Miss Adele couldn't find a studio in Battery Park for eight hundred grand you're crazy. If she had any genius at all, it was for real estate.)

Sweating with effort and anxiety, Miss Adele got stuck at her middle section, which had become, somehow, Devin's middle section. Her fingers fumbled with the heavy-duty eyes and hooks. She found she was breathing heavily. ABOMIN-ATION, yelled the radio. *Get it out of my store!* cried the man, in all likelihood. *Have mercy!* pleaded the woman, basically. That thirty per cent of extra Devin-schlub had replicated itself exactly around her own once-lovely waist. No matter how she pulled she simply could not contain it. So much effort! She could hear herself making odd noises, grunts almost.

'Hey, you okay in there?'

'First doesn't work. Trying the second.'

'No, don't do that. Wait. Wendy, get in there.'

In a second the girl was in front of her, and as close as anybody had been to Miss Adele's bare body in a long time. Without a word, a little hand reached out for the corset, took hold of one side of it and, with surprising strength, pulled it towards the other end until both sides met. The girl nodded, and this was Miss Adele's cue to hook the thing together while the girl squatted like a weightlifter and took a series of short, fierce breaths. Outside of the curtain, the argument had resumed.

'Breathe,' said the girl.

'They always talk to each other like that?' asked Miss Adele.

The girl looked up, uncomprehending.

'Okay now?'

'Sure. Thanks.'

The girl ducked out. Miss Adele examined her new

silhouette. It was as good as it was going to get. She turned to the side and frowned at three days of chest stubble. In winter certain grooming habits became hard to keep up. She pulled her shirt over her head to see the clothed effect from the opposite angle and, in the transition, got a fresh view of the husband, still berating Mrs Alexander, though now in a violent whisper. At the same moment, he seemed to become aware of being observed and looked up at Miss Adele – not as far as her eyes, but tracing, from the neck down, the contours of her body. RIGHTEOUSNESS, cried the radio, RIGHTEOUS-NESS AND RAGE! Miss Adele felt like a nail being hammered into the floor. She grabbed the curtain and yanked it shut. She heard the husband end the conversation abruptly – as had been her own father's way – not with reason or persuasion, but sheer volume. Above the door to the emporium, the little bell rang.

'Molly! So good to see you! How're the kids? I'm just with a customer!' Mrs Alexander's long pale fingers curled round the hem of the velvet. 'May I?'

Miss Adele opened the curtain.

'Oh, it's good! See, you got shape now.'

Miss Adele shrugged, dangerously close to tears: 'It works.'

'Good. Marcus said it would work. He can spot a corset size at forty paces, believe me. He's good for that at least. So, if that works, the other will work. Why not take both? Then you don't have to come back for another twenty years! It's a bargain. Molly, I'm right with you.'

In the store there had appeared a gaggle of children, small and large, and two motherly-looking women, who were greeting the husband and being greeted warmly in turn, smiled at, kissed on both cheeks, et cetera. Miss Adele picked up her enormous coat and began the process of re-weatherizing herself. She observed Mrs Alexander's husband reaching over the counter to joke with two young children, ruffling their hair, while his wife – whom she watched even more intently – stood over this phoney operation, smiling, as if all that had passed between him and her were nothing at all, only a little domestic incident, some silly wrangle about the accounts, or whatnot. Oh, Loretta Young. Whatever you need to tell yourself. Family first! A phrase that sounded, to Miss Adele, so broad, so empty; one of those convenient pits into which folk will throw any and every thing they can't deal with alone. A hole for cowards to hide in. So you could have your hands round your wife's throat, you could have your terrified little boys cowering in a corner – but when the bell rings, it's time for tea and 'Family First!', with the congregants as your audience, and Mamma's cakes, and smiles all round. *These are my sons, Devin and Darren.* Two shows a day for seventeen years. Once you've seen behind the curtain, you can never look at it the same way again.

Miss Adele stared-down a teenage girl leaning on the counter, who now remembered her manners, looked away and closed her mouth. 'Can I ask you a question?' she asked Mrs Alexander as she approached, carrying two corsets packed back into their boxes. 'You got kids?'

'Five!'

Miss Adele felt exhausted. She had read in *The Times* that by 2050 most of the city would be single-occupant households. Which was meant to be bad news somehow.

'Jesus Christ,' she said.

'No,' said Mrs Alexander, rubbing her chin thoughtfully. 'He was definitely not involved. I'll be with you in one minute,

Sarah! It's been so –' She broke off to snap violently at her husband, and to be snapped at in return, before seamlessly returning to her sentence. '*Long*. So long! And look at these girls! They're really tall now!'

Miss Adele took the corsets and reached for her wallet.

'Sorry, but am I causing you some kind of issue? I mean, between you and your . . .'

Both women looked over at the husband, who did not look up, for he was busy fussing with the radio's antenna as the shouting sputtered into static.

'You?' said Mrs Alexander, and with so innocent a face Miss Adele was tempted to award her the Oscar right there and then, though it was only February. 'How do you mean, issue?'

Miss Adele smiled.

'You should be on the stage. You could be my warm-up act.'

'Oh, I doubt you need much warming – even in these temperatures. No, you don't pay me, you pay him.' A small child ran by Mrs Alexander with a pink bra on his head. Without a word she lifted it, folded it in half and tucked the straps neatly within the cups. 'You got kids?'

Miss Adele was so surprised, so utterly wrong-footed by this question, she found herself speaking the truth.

'My twin – he does. He has kids. We're identical twins. I guess I feel like his kids are mine, too.'

Mrs Alexander put her hands on her tiny waist and shook her head.

'Now, that is *fascinating*. You know, I never thought of that before. Genetics is an amazing thing – amazing! If I wasn't in the corset business, I'm telling you, that would have been my line. Better luck next time, right?' She laughed sadly, and looked over at the counter. 'He listens to his lectures all day, he's educated. I missed out on all that. Okay, so – are we happy?'

Are *you* happy? Are you really happy, Loretta Young? Would you tell me if you weren't, Loretta Young, the Bishop's Wife? Oh, Loretta Young, Loretta Young! Would you tell anybody?

'Molly, don't say another word – I know exactly what you need. Nice meeting you,' said Mrs Alexander to Miss Adele, over her shoulder, as she took her new customer behind the curtain. 'If you go over to my husband, you can settle up with him. Have a good day.'

Miss Adele approached the counter and placed her corsets upon it. She looked hard at the side of Mrs Alexander's husband's head. He picked up the first box. He looked at it as if he'd never seen a corset box before. Slowly he wrote something down in a notepad in front of him. He picked up the second and repeated the procedure, but with even less haste. Then, without looking up, he pushed both boxes to his left, until they reached the hands of the shop girl, Wendy.

'Forty-six fifty,' said Wendy, though she didn't sound very sure. 'Um . . . Mr Alexander – is there discount on Paramount?'

He was in his own world, staring straight ahead. Wendy let a finger brush the boss's sleeve; it seemed to waken him from his stupor. Suddenly he sat very tall on his stool and thumped a fist upon the counter – just like Daddy casting out the Devil over breakfast – and started right back up shouting at his wife, it was some form of stinging question, which he repeated over and over, in that relentless way these men always have. Miss Adele strained to understand it. Something like: *You happy* now? Or: *Is this what you want?* Or: *See what you've done? See what you've done? See what you've done?*

'Hey, you,' said Miss Adele, 'yes, you, sir. If I'm so disgusting to you? If I'm so beneath your contempt? Why're you taking my money? Huh? You're going to take my money? *My* money? Then, please: look me in the eye. Do me that favour, okay? Look me in the eye.'

Very slowly a pair of blue eyes rose to meet Miss Adele's own green contacts. The blue was unexpected, like the inner markings of some otherwise unremarkable butterfly, and the black lashes were wet and long and trembling. His voice too, was the opposite of his wife's, slow and deliberate, as if each word had been weighed against eternity before being chosen for use.

'You are speaking to me?'

'Yes, I'm speaking to you. I'm talking about customer service. Customer service. Ever hear of it? I am your customer. And I don't appreciate being treated like something you picked up on your damn shoe!'

The husband sighed and rubbed at his left eye.

'I don't understand – I say something to you? My wife, she say something to you?'

Miss Adele shifted her weight to her other hip and very briefly considered a retreat. It did sometimes happen, after all – she knew from experience – that is, when you spent a good amount of time alone – it did sometimes come to pass – when trying to decipher the signals of others – that sometimes you mistook –

'Listen, your wife is friendly – she's civilized, I'm not talking about your wife. I'm talking about *you*. Listening to your . . . I don't know what – your *hate speech* – blasting through this store. You may not think I'm godly, brother, and maybe I'm not, but I am in your store with good old-fashioned American money and I ask that you respect that and you respect me.'

He began on his other eye, same routine.

'I see,' he said, eventually.

'Excuse me?'

'You understand what is being said, on this radio?'

'*What?*'

'You speak this language that you hear on the radio?'

'I don't *need* to speak it to understand it. And why you got it turned up to eleven? I'm a customer – whatever's being said, I don't want to listen to that shit. I don't need a translation – I can hear the *tone*. And don't think I don't see the way you're look-ing at me. You want to tell your wife about that? When you were peeping at me through that curtain?'

'First you say I'm not looking at you. Now I'm looking at you?'

'Is there a problem?' said Mrs Alexander. Her head came out from behind the curtain.

'I'm not an idiot,' said Miss Adele. She flicked the radio's cas-ing with a finger. 'I got radar for this shit. And you and I both know there's a way of not looking at somebody that is looking at them.'

The husband brought his hands together, somewhere between prayer and exasperation, and shook them at his wife as he spoke to her, over Miss Adele's head, and around her comprehension.

'Hey – talk in English. English! Don't disrespect me! Speak in English!'

'Let me translate for you: I am asking my wife what she did to upset you.'

Miss Adele turned and saw Mrs Alexander, clinging to herself and swaying, less like Loretta now, more like Vivien Leigh swearing on the red earth of Tara.

'I'm not talking about her!'

'Sir, was I not polite and friendly to you? Sir?'

'First up, I ain't no sir — you live in this city, use the right words for the right shit, okay?'

There was Miss Adele's temper, bad as ever. She'd always had it. Even before she was Miss Adele, when she was still little Darren Bailey, it had been a problem. Had a tendency to go off whenever she was on uncertain ground, like a poorly set firework, exploding in odd, unpredictable directions, hurting innocent bystanders — often women, for some reason. How many women had stood opposite Miss Adele with the exact same look on their faces as Mrs Alexander wore right now? Starting with her mother and stretching way out to the horizon. The only Judgement Day that had ever made sense to Miss Adele was the one where all the hurt and disappointed ladies form a line — a chorus line of hurt feelings — and one by one, give you your pedigree, over and over, for all eternity.

'Was I rude to you?' asked Mrs Alexander, the colour rising in her face. 'No, I was not. I live, I let live.'

Miss Adele looked around at her audience. Everybody in the store had stopped what they were doing and fallen silent.

'I'm not talking to you. I'm trying to talk to this gentleman here. Could you turn off that radio so I can talk to you, please?'

'Okay, so maybe you leave now,' he said.

'Second of all,' said Miss Adele, counting it out on her hand, though there was nothing to follow in the list. 'Contrary to appearances, and just as a point of information, I am not an Arab.

Oh, I know I look like an Arab. Long nose. Pale. People always getting that shit twisted. So you can hate me, fine – but you should know who you're hating and hate me for the right reasons. Because right now? You're hating in the wrong direction – you and your radio are wasting your hate. If you want to hate me, file it under N-word. As in African-American. Yeah.'

The husband frowned and held his beard in his hand.

'You are a very confused person. The truth is I don't care what you are. All such conversations are very boring to me, in fact.'

As if he *knew* boredom was the purest form of aggression to Miss Adele! She who had always been so beautiful and so fascinating – she who had never known ambivalence!

'Oh, I'm *boring* you?'

'Honestly, yes. And you are also being quite rude. So now I ask politely: leave, please.'

'I am out that door, believe me. I can't fucking *wait* to stop listening to that noise. But I am *not* leaving without my mother-fucking corset.'

The husband slipped off his stool, finally, and stood up.

'You leave now, please.'

'Who's gonna make me? You can't touch me, right? That's one of your laws, right? I'm unclean, right? So who's gonna touch me? Miss Tiny Exploited Migrant Worker over here?'

'Hey, fuck you, racist asshole! I'm international student! NYU!'

Et tu, Wendy? Miss Adele looked sadly at her would-be ally. Wendy was a whole foot taller now, thanks to the stepladder, and she was using the opportunity to point a finger in Miss Adele's face. Tired to death.

'Just give me my damn corset.'

'Sir, I'm sorry but you really have to leave now,' said Mrs Alexander, walking towards Miss Adele, her elegant arms wrapped around her itty-bitty waist. 'There are minors in here, and your language is not appropriate.'

'Y'all call me "sir" one more time,' said Miss Adele, speaking to Mrs Alexander, but still looking at the husband, 'I'm gonna throw that radio right out that fucking window. And don't you be thinking I'm an anti-Semite or some shit . . .' Miss Adele faded. She had the out-of-body sense that she was watching herself on the big screen, at one of those Chelsea screenings she used to attend, with a beloved boy, long dead, who'd adored shouting at the screen, back when that was even a thing. When young people still went to see old movies in a cinema. Oh, if that boy were alive! If he could see Miss Adele up on that screen right now! Wouldn't he be shouting at her performance – wouldn't he groan and cover his eyes! The way he did at Hedy or Ava as they made their terrible life choices, all of them unalterable, no matter how loudly you shouted. The boy was not alive. He couldn't shout or put his head on Miss Adele's shoulder, and no one had, or ever could, replace him, and these new boys you met found the old movies 'camp' and 'embarrassing', and Devin had his own life – his kids, his wife – and there was no home any more beyond 10th Street.

'It's a question,' stated Miss Adele, 'of simple politeness. Po-lite-ness.'

The husband shook his shaggy head and laughed, softly.

'You're being polite? Is this polite?'

'But I didn't start this –'

'Incorrect. You started it.'

'You're trying to act like I'm crazy, but from the moment I stepped up in here, you been trying to make me feel like you don't want someone like me up in here – why you even denying it? You can't even look at me now! I know you hate black people. I know you hate homosexual people. You think I don't know that? I can look at you and know that.'

'But you're wrong!' cried the wife.

'No, Eleanor, maybe she's right,' said the husband, putting out a hand to stop the wife continuing. 'Maybe she sees into the hearts of men.'

'You know what? It's obvious this lady can't speak for herself when you're around. I don't even want to talk about this another second. My money's on the counter. This is twenty-first-century New York. This is America. And I've paid for my goods. Give me my goods.'

'Take your money and leave. I ask you politely. Before I call the police.'

'I'm sure he'll go peacefully,' predicted Mrs Alexander, tearing the nail of her index finger between her teeth, but, instead, one more thing went wrong in Miss Adele's mind, and she grabbed that corset right out of Mrs Alexander's husband's hands, kicked the door of Clinton Corset Emporium wide open and high-tailed it down the freezing street, slipped on some ice and went down pretty much face first. After which, well, she had some regrets, sure, but there wasn't much else to do at that point but pick herself up and run, with a big, bleeding dramatic gash all along her left cheek, wig askew, surely looking to everyone she passed exactly like some Bellevue psychotic, a hot crazy mess, an old-school deviant from the fabled city of the past – except, every soul on these streets was a stranger to Miss Adele. They didn't have the context, didn't know a damn thing about where she was coming from, nor that she'd paid for her goods in full, in dirty green American dollars, and was only taking what was rightfully hers.

the riddle of . . . thing, and wisdom finally answered . . .

Mood

Time

There's no woodland or forest-like aspect but it does feel like the middle of something, and wisdom finally arrives, even if only as an awareness that inside the adult flesh cages lurk the exact same children. By the time you've come to grips with January it's already April and that's all a year actually *is* – a series of months that jump four at a time – so it's three leaps to the end of the year and that sad annual pretence that anyone might actually go anywhere New Year's Eve. Then it's April again. The dogs are shitting on the Mercer Street daffodils, and Mary Baker Eddy (of MacDougal Street) still hasn't managed to diarize a single dinner date with Siddartha (corner of 15th and Sixth). Whither enlightenment? You see the dazed city people, opening those big, blue, unused and unloved street-corner mailboxes, their heads stuffed right down the chutes, feet dangling off the ground, looking for something they've lost, namely, the summer of their ninth year, which stretched from the early 1600s until approximately the Korean War. What a cosmic joke! There's not even anything original about this malaise: all the citizens of late capitalism feel exactly the same way about time. End scene.

Roberta

Whatever happens to old punks? Enquiring minds want to know. Well, I can be very precise about it because I happen to know Roberta, once the door bitch at CBGB's. Roberta knew Ms Harry and she knew the Ramones – they often swapped clothes – and she took the best photographs of the scene in the East Village at that time and must have partaken of a bit of smack back in the day but I dare you to ask her. Now she's Queen of the Dog Park and we hail her! We hail, too, her little pug Edie who sits on a bench with the humans, wrapped in a mink stole, taking a dim view of her own kind. Old punks wear all black, they are covered in dog hair, their own hair is purple, they really do not suffer fools, they are unimpressed by all impressive things, they worship pugs above people and pity fans who have only graves and Houston Street murals to visit. Old punks have succeeded in staying alive and remaining rent-controlled. They do not complain about the changing city because only bougie cunts do that. They attend pug meets. They unironically admire the withered pug in the home-made wheelchair, dragging the weight of himself around the room. Irony in general means nothing to old punks; they consider it too distant from blood, bile, phlegm and black bile. HOWEVER. They are not above attending an exhibit about Richard Hell at the Brooklyn Museum should such an exhibition come to pass. Unexpectedly, Joan Crawford's autobiography serves as a personal bible. Nightly services are held throughout the East Village while lounging in bed watching TCM. Surviving punks WhatsApp each other throughout whichever movie, smoking their own marijuana. 'What is *wrong* with Esther Williams?' 'Collapsed vulva.'

Old punks, having survived all the parties, now prefer parties for one. Do not imagine that because you got commissioned for a second series or are presently showing in some blue-chip gallery in Chelsea that any of this means anything whatsoever to Roberta – she remains a door bitch. The order of business is:

1. Charm of dog
2. Psychology of dog
3. Behaviour of dog
4. Humour/moods of dog

This list goes on for a good long while before personhood becomes an issue. Crawford herself couldn't get through that gate without a dog. When old punks don't win the fancy-dress contest – despite presenting four different pugs dressed as sushi rolls sitting on a bed of nori – old punks can become enraged, filled with black bile, and will make their contempt for the Friends of Washington Square Association perfectly clear. The glorious essence of punk remains a refusal to be cowed, most especially by time. But even Roberta was a little unnerved to see her long-term parrot, Preston, pass from this world into the world beyond, the one to which we are all finally heading, hidden behind the beaded curtain, out of view, where all the comic books, hookahs, lip rings and bad tattoos are stored. Is it still punk to be predeceased by a parrot?

The Black Market

I said to Raphael, I said: 'I'm going to quote Du Bois at you. I'm going to say: *How does it feel to be a problem?*'

And Raphael said: 'Right, except if it was also and at the same time: *How does it feel to be a sensation?*'

The answer is: still not really like a person.

Raphael is very beautiful and stylish, but he doesn't over-dress like a fashion student; he dresses with the good taste of someone who until recently was not fired by Frieze for calling a senior editor a 'zombie collector whore'. (Mitigating circumstances: Raphael's yearly wage was thirteen thousand dollars.) He's moved from Bushwick to Forest Hills. Back up in the mix with his tote bag. But he is feeling the general malaise. Feels like he's being 'torn apart inside'. Raphael takes wonderful photographs of black skin but now everybody's doing that, you literally can't move for photos of the 'black body' and he was more interested in one particular black body (his own) but it's this generalized 'black body' they're all looking for now, and you get paid on a rising scale for how much white guilt you can squeeze out of a pound of flesh, and this is very tempting, extremely tempting, but Raphael is of the older generation (twenty-five) and is awful close to going offline altogether, or at least removing himself from every platform, because holy God it is *exhausting*. (Out of nostalgia for his youth, however, Raphael will be staying on Tumblr.) The struggle, the hustle, the struggle, the hustle, the struggle, the hustle! The intended audience can't usually tell the difference between these two, but those in the know know what they know. All of which means nobody's in the market for these exquisite pictures of Raphael's face at the moment of orgasm, and that's a damn shame. 'There's these doors opening up all over the place but the catch is they only open if you lie on the floor and start performatively bleeding.' His boo meanwhile is nineteen, white, walking for Versace in Milan at this moment, this very moment, which also involves more than a pound of flesh – Struggle! Hustle! – but 'he's a big boy and he knows what he's getting into'.

The older people in this city appear to be eating the younger ones alive.

'Yes, yes,' said Raphael, putting his feet up on my desk, 'but that's my point: maybe it's time for me to become the diner instead of the meal! I'm beautiful! I'm talented! I've got something to say!'

It was actually my office hours and Raphael is not a student of mine so we laughed at ourselves and gazed out of the window towards the tip of the island. That's where the boats come in every second Tuesday from every part of the country and armies of young people dressed like sailors – like Gene Kelly in *On the Town* – run up the gangplank, stretch out their arms to the city and sing: 'I'm beautiful! I'm talented! I've got something to say!' And they're all right, every single one of them.

Locate the Self

Are you in your tote bag? In the plants? In the bad faith soda-stream (Palestinian tears)? In your rug? In the city's half-assed attempt to recycle? In your children? In your decision not to have children? In your tribe? In your kink? In your place of employment? In your wage packet? In the likes? In the rejections? In your documentation? In this sentence? Relatively recently a man called Leopold and a woman called Kwa could walk into the cleared central areas of their respective villages and locate themselves very firmly between their cottage/*mousgoum* and their church/elders circle, and the river/desert and the hills/mountains. Moods were collective yet circumscribed; one put one's mood in the service of the group; there were seasons of moods and places to have them, and the work of managing moods was never left to any one body alone because no one could imagine that a single consciousness could ever process or contain all the moods that there are on this earth without feeling like they were being 'torn apart inside'. (Possession, zombies, speaking in tongues, exorcism, automatons, uncanny valleys, body-snatching, devil-control, hoodoo.)

Moods on Tumblr

probably unpopular opinion, but I rly hate those posts that are like "americans who say they are x ethnicity will never be accepted by people from x country! they aren't really x!"

hello im making this text post since apparently some of you guys have the same amount of manners as a slab of concrete which is none at all

DONT ADD YOUR WEIRDO COMMENTS ON PEOPLES ART. christ.

spicy take
 a lot of people on here irrationally hate this show because they

conflate its criticism with the way capitalism uses technology with "durr technology is bad fire is scary and thomas edison was a witch".

I really hate it when goyim use the word Zionist because

okay let's talk: i'm writing this because 1) i don't mind being blunt, and 2) i'm more than a little sick and tired of seeing others get taken advantage of or be made anxious.

so today i'm yelling about

UNCOMFORTABLE WRITING TRUTHS

The Top Ten Worst Things to Say to an Autistic Person

Oh Hell No . . . . .

WE NEED TO TALK: Just because a character is showing emotions and they are portrayed *sympathetically* or they do something *relatable* or "*human*" does NOT automatically translate into = "Redemption"

You are all terrible, you know that?

Okay so . . . here's the part where I explain to people who don't understand how WORDS work . . . .

First of all . . . . you can try and put words into my mouth ALL you like . . . . You can fuck off too . . . . I'm an AMERICAN I'm calling out the hateful people I see all the time.

The letter Ricardo wrote to his girlfriend for Valentine's Day 2018, the day he was murdered.

Part of me fighting my constant self hate shit was stepping back, realizing I was comparing myself to other people and that it was unhealthy, and then sitting down and listing out the things I thought were cool about the other person without judgement.

I'll give you a tip about adulting: you don't have to adult the same way other adults adult.

Tall bottoms are the most oppressed members of the gay community.

You'll never be bored again.
You'll never be bored again.
You'll never be bored again.

Absurd Modern Mood

'And the crazy thing is,' said the Professor of the Philosophy of History to the Professor of the History of Philosophy, 'how difficult an *easy* life is! I mean, imagine what a *difficult* life feels like!'

A nearby graduate, Zenobia, presently assembling a sly dinner out of Philosophy Department canapés – while simultaneously trying to disguise the look of actual hunger in her eyes – took a moment. Suddenly she was overcome by the sense that none of this was real. Not the canapés, not the professors, not the Philosophy Department, nor the whole city campus. (Zenobia has ninety-six thousand dollars in loans. She is studying Philosophy, period.)

Medieval Moods: Blood, Black Bile, Bile, Phlegm

To leave Monrovia while six months pregnant and lightly spotting, and then to head to Libya, reaching its coast when you are eight months pregnant and bleeding more steadily, where you then launch yourself out to sea, in a small dinghy, stuffed with eighty other people, heading for Lampedusa – in that situation it will certainly help to be bloody, and therefore sanguine, though with a touch of black bile, which will make you goal-orientated and determined.

To separate an un-potty-trained four-year-old from its mother at the border and place it in confinement, with several other children of similar age, and a crate of Pampers, as if you hope the children will figure out how to change themselves, and then to walk past the visiting nurse and social worker with lowered eyes as you three pass each other at the tent flap, because none of you can quite stand to look at each other – to perform this action it is essential that you have phlegm and are phlegmatic in general, so that you can be good at generalizing ideas or problems in the world and making compromises.

If your great-grandparents were sharecroppers, and you're the first of your clan to attend university, and you are interested in the philosophy of the self, and your dream is to be a photographer, and you are studying in the hope of achieving your goal, but by graduation you will owe a hundred and thirty thousand dollars in student loans – in this case you will develop a melancholy strain of bile, which manifests itself in a strive for perfection, which other, less sensitive people, like your room-mates, will experience as irritating, and diagnose as OCD, citing as evidence your tendency not to be able to leave the apartment until all the knobs on the cooker are facing north and the cheap, plastic blinds are partially raised to the exact same height to let the light through.

When a beloved parrot dies? Melancholy, forsooth, only melancholy.

Roberta and Preston (A Dialogue)

Roberta (reading from the paper):
      They're saying it's made almost no difference.

Preston: That's a laugh!

Roberta: It doesn't matter what he does, because it's not rational, it's emotional.

Preston: That's a laugh!

Roberta: Except it's not very funny.

Preston: *Twenty-ee-ee-five hours to go! I wanna be sedated!*

Roberta: I'm being serious. They're still behind him. He makes them feel good. They want him to just go ahead and shoot somebody on Fifth Avenue like he promised.

Preston: *I wanna be sedated! I wanna be sedated!*

Roberta: Okay, okay, okay . . . Did I feed Edie? Did you see me feed Edie? Did Edie already eat?

Preston: That's a laugh!

Roberta (closing the paper):
          Well, if we're lucky maybe one of us will drop dead off our perch before 2020.

Preston (under his breath):
          Lord, let it be me.

All the Moods vs the Individual

Zenobia was dog-sitting for the photographer lady downstairs, who had travelled to Pennsylvania to bury her parrot in a famous pet cemetery. It was an opportunity to see the apartment. What was amazing about the apartments of long-standing adults was the accumulation of incidental texture. Not: *I went and bought this lamp and this poster so I would have a lamp and a poster to furnish my life*. But just stuff, so much stuff everywhere, somehow the consequence of a certain amount of time on earth. For her Tumblr (entirely unfollowed), Zenobia photographed:

36 DVD cases of old movies two thirds of which were empty

A gypsy shawl hung over a lamp waiting to burn down the whole building

A large black dildo standing proud on a side table and signed in silver Sharpie by someone apparently un-Googleable

Four pairs of red silk Chinese slippers, very beautiful

A little pyramid of dog hair on the windowsill

All around the apartment were photographs taken by the tenant, extraordinary photographs of old punks when young – stylish, smart, daring, strikingly composed photographs, taken on a real camera – but Zenobia found herself unable to photograph them. Just looking at them was hard enough. She fed Edie, remembering to hide the pill in the wet food and separate wet from dry. She lay on the floor. Her new Liberian twists fanned out around her head. She tried to muster the energy to lift her phone to her eyes and thus locate herself in the online DSM. Edie shuffled by, paying Zenobia no mind. For half a century, 'feeling unreal' was known as DPD (De-personalization Disorder), but has recently been renamed and recategorized as DDD (De-personalization/De-realization Disorder) which refers not only to the feeling of personal unreality but also to the sense that the world around you likewise does not exist. Near-sighted Edie – who like many pugs of her age suffered from retinal damage – moseyed back round the way she'd came, paused at Zenobia's face, and licked her right in the nostril.

Locate the Self II

Find a Grave   . . . . .   search name

West End, Section 36, plot B71
Name: "Preston"
Breed: Parrot, African Grey
Headstone: Preston 1970–2019 *"Everybody has a Poison Heart"*

Mood Memory

The phone book was an annual April excitement, arriving in bound stacks of four, bright yellow. You looked up kids you fancied, or notorious bitches and bullies, and sought out tragic last names – Cock, Bumstead – to see if any such people existed and where they lived. One trickster of a teacher swore to us that his real first name was Rover – his parents had wanted a dog – and everybody laughed and no one believed him, but then he said go on and look it up in the phone book and that's what we did, me and my brother, and there it was, Rover! Magic. That's what everyone's looking for down those stupid mail chutes but it doesn't come again, or not quite in that form.

My father was always threatening to unlist us, because he shared a name with a famous jockey and strangers would periodically call the flat to ask him which horse they should bet on in the Grand National. We begged him not to unlist us. We wanted to locate ourselves. We flicked excitedly through the pages, thin like onion skin, yellow, easily torn, and landed with delight on the most common surname in England and said oh there we are there we are there we are there we are there we are

Escape From New York

It had been a very long time since he'd been responsible for another human. Never had he organized travel for himself or anybody. But it was his fault they were all three in the city, and so it fell to him. There was perhaps even something a little exciting about discovering, for the first time in his life, that he was not useless, that his father was wrong, and in fact he was capable. He called Elizabeth first.

'I'm in a state of terror,' Elizabeth said.

'Wait,' Michael said, hearing a beep on the line. 'Let me bring in Marlon.'

'The world's gone crazy!' Elizabeth said. 'I can't even believe what I'm looking at!'

'Hi, Marlon,' Michael said.

'So – where are we?' Marlon said.

'"*Where are we?*"' Elizabeth said. 'We're in a state of terror, that's where we are.'

'We're all right,' Marlon grumbled. He sounded far away. 'We'll handle it.'

Michael could hear Marlon's TV in the background. It was tuned to the same channel Michael was watching, but only Michael could see the images on the screen replicated simultaneously through his own window, a strange doubling sensation, like when you stand on a stage and look up at yourself on the JumboTron. Elizabeth and Marlon were staying uptown; normally Michael, too, would be staying uptown – until five days ago he'd almost never set foot below 42nd Street. Everyone – his brothers and sisters, all his West Coast friends – had warned him not to go downtown. It's dangerous downtown, it's always been that way, just stick with what you know, stay at the Carlyle. But because the helipad near the Garden had, for some reason, been out of commission it had been decided he should stay downtown, for reasons of proximity and to avoid traffic. Now Michael looked south and saw a sky darkened with ash. The ash seemed to be moving toward him. Downtown was really so much worse than anyone in LA could even begin to imagine.

'Some things you *can't* handle,' Elizabeth said. 'I'm in a state of terror.'

'There are no flights allowed,' Michael said, trying to feel capable, filling them in. 'No one can charter. Not even the very important people.'

'Bullshit!' Marlon said. 'You think Weinstein's not on a plane right now? You think Eisner's not on a plane?'

'Marlon, in case you've forgotten,' Elizabeth said, 'I am also a Jew. Am I on a plane, Marlon? Am I on a plane?'

Marlon groaned. 'Oh, for Chrissake. I didn't mean it that way.'

'Well, how the hell *did* you mean it?'

Michael bit his lip. The truth was, these two dear friends of his were both closer friends to him than they were to each other, and there were often these awkward moments when he had to remind them of the love thread that connected all three, which, to Michael, was so obvious; it was woven from a shared suffering, a unique form of suffering, that few people on this earth have ever known or will ever have the chance to experience, but which all of them – Michael, Liz, and Marlon – happened to have undergone to the highest degree possible. As Marlon sometimes said, 'The only other guy who knew what this feels like got nailed to a couple of planks of wood!' Sometimes, if Elizabeth wasn't around, he would add, 'By the Jews,' but Michael tried not to linger on these aspects of Marlon, preferring to remember the love thread, for that was all that really mattered, in the end. 'I think what Marlon meant –' Michael began, but Marlon cut him off: 'Let's focus here! We've got to focus!'

'We can't fly,' Michael said quietly. 'I don't know why, really. That's just what they're saying.'

'I'm packing,' Elizabeth said, and down the line came the sound of something precious smashing on the floor. 'I don't even know what I'm packing, but I'm packing.'

'Let's be rational about this,' Marlon said. 'There's a lot of car services. I can't think of any right now. On TV you see them. They've got all kinds of names. Hertz? That's one. There must be others.'

'I am truly in a state of terror,' Elizabeth said.

'You said that already!' Marlon shouted. 'Get ahold of yourself!'

'I'll try and call a car place,' Michael said. 'The phones down here are kind of screwy.' On a pad he wrote, *Hurts*.

'Essentials only,' Marlon said, referring to Liz's packing. 'This is not the fucking *QE2*. This is not fucking cocktail hour with good old Dick up in St. Moritz. Essentials.'

'It'll be a big car,' Michael murmured. He hated arguments.

'It'll sure as hell have to be,' Elizabeth said, and Michael knew she was being sarcastic and referring to Marlon's weight. Marlon knew it, too. The line went silent. Michael bit his lip some more. He could see in the vanity mirror that his lip looked very red, but then he remembered that he had permanently tattooed it that colour.

'Elizabeth, listen to me,' Marlon said, in his angry but controlled mumble, which gave Michael an inappropriate little thrill; he couldn't help it, it was just such classic Marlon. 'Put that goddamn Krupp on your pinkie and let's get the fuck out of here.'

Marlon hung up.

Elizabeth started crying. There was a beep on the line.

'I should probably take that,' Michael said.

At noon, Michael put on his usual disguise and picked up the car in an underground garage near Herald Square. At 12.27 p.m., he pulled up in front of the Carlyle.

'Jesus Christ that was fast,' Marlon said. He was sitting on the sidewalk, on one of those portable collapsible chairs you sometimes see people bring along when they camp outside your hotel all night in the hope that you'll step out onto the balcony and wave to them. He wore a funny bucket hat like a fisherman's, elasticated sweatpants, and a huge Hawaiian shirt.

'I took the superfast river road!' Michael said. He didn't mean to look too smug about it, given the context, but he couldn't help but be a little bit proud.

Marlon opened a carton he had on his lap and took out a cheeseburger. He eyed the vehicle.

'I hear you drive like a maniac.'

'I do go fast, Marlon, but I also stay in control. You can trust me, Marlon. I promise I will get us out of here.'

Michael felt really sad seeing Marlon like that, eating a cheeseburger on the sidewalk. He was so fat, and his little chair was under a lot of strain. The whole situation looked very precarious. This was also the moment when he noticed that Marlon wasn't wearing any shoes.

'Have you seen Liz?' Michael asked.

'What *is* that hunk of junk, anyway?' Marlon asked.

Michael had forgotten. He leaned over and took the manual out of the glove compartment.

'A Toyota Camry. It's all they had.' He was about to add 'with a roomy back seat' but thought better of it.

'The Japanese are a wise people,' Marlon said. Behind Marlon, the doors of the Carlyle opened and a bellboy emerged walking backward with a tower of Louis Vuitton luggage on a trolley and Elizabeth at his side. She was wearing a lot of diamonds: several necklaces, bracelets up her arms, and a mink stole covered with so many brooches it looked like a pin cushion.

'You have got to be kidding me,' Marlon said.

A logician? A negotiator? Michael did not usually have much call to think of himself in this way. But now, back on the road and speeding toward Bethlehem, he allowed the thought that people had always overjudged and misunderestimated him and maybe in the end you don't really know a person until that person is truly tested by a big event, like the apocalypse. Of course, people forgot he'd been raised a Witness. In one way or another, he'd been expecting this day for a long, long time. Still, if anyone had told him, twenty-four hours ago, that he would be able to convince Elizabeth – she who once bought a seat on a plane for a dress so it could meet her in Istanbul – to join him on an escape from New York, in a funky old Japanese car, abandoning five of her Louis Vuitton cases to a city under attack, well, he truly wouldn't have believed it. Who knew he had such powers of persuasion? He'd never had to persuade anyone of anything, least of all his own genius, which was, of course, a weird childhood gift he'd never asked for and which had proved impossible to give back. Maybe even harder was getting Marlon to agree that they would not stop again for food until they hit Pennsylvania. He leaned forward to see if there were any more enemy combatants in the sky. There were not. He and his friends were really escaping! He had taken control and was making the right decisions for everybody! He looked across at Liz, in the passenger seat: she was calm, at last, but her eyeliner continued to run down her beautiful face. So much eyeliner. Everything Michael knew about eyeliner he'd learned from Liz, but now he realized he had something to teach *her* on the subject: make it permanent. Tattoo it right around the tear ducts. That way, it never runs.

'Am I losing my mind?' Marlon asked. 'Or did you say Bethlehem?'

Michael adjusted the rear-view mirror until he could see Marlon, stretched out on the back seat, reading a book and breaking into the emergency Twinkies, which Michael thought they had all agreed to save till Allentown.

'It's a town in Pennsylvania,' Michael said. 'We'll stop there, eat, and then we'll go again.'

'Are you *reading*?' Elizabeth asked. 'How can you be reading at this moment?'

'What should I be doing?' Marlon enquired, somewhat testily. 'Shakespeare in the Park?'

'I just don't understand how a person can be reading when their country is under attack. We could all die at any moment.'

'If you'd read your Sartre, honey, you'd know that was true at all times in all situations.'

Elizabeth scowled and folded her twinkling hands in her lap. 'I just don't see how a person can read at such a time.'

'Well, *Liz*,' Marlon said, laying it on thick, 'let me enlighten you. See, I guess I read because I am what you'd call a reader. Because I am interested in *the life of the mind*. I admit it. I don't even have a screening room: no, instead I have a library. Imagine that! Imagine that! Because it happens that my highest calling in life is not to put my fat little hands in a pile of sandy shit outside Grauman's –'

'Oh, brother, here we go.'

'Because I actually aspire to comprehend the ways and inclinations of the human –'

'These people are trying to kill us!' Liz screamed, and Michael felt it was really time to intervene.

'Not *us*,' he ventured. 'I guess, like, not *especially* us.' But then a thought came to him. 'Elizabeth, you don't think . . . ?'

He had not thought this thought until now – he had been too busy with logistics – but now he began to think it. And he could tell everyone else in the car was thinking it, too.

'How would I know?' Liz cried, twisting her biggest ring around her smallest finger. 'Maybe! First the financial centres, then the government folks, and then –'

'The very important people,' Michael whispered.

'Wouldn't be at all surprised,' Marlon said, turning solemn.

'We're exactly the kinds of sons of bitches who'd make a nice trophy on some crazy motherfucker's wall.'

He sounded scared, at last. And hearing Marlon scared made Michael as scared as he'd been all day. You never want to see your father scared, or your mother cry, and, as far as Michael's chosen family went, that's exactly what was happening right now, in this bad Japanese car that did not smell of new leather or new anything. It made him wish he'd tried harder to bring Liza along. On the other hand, maybe that would have been worse. It was almost as if his chosen family were as crushing to his emotional health as his real family! And that thought was really not one that he could allow himself to have on this day of all days – on any day.

'We're all under a lot of strain,' Michael said. His voice was a little wobbly, but he didn't worry about crying; that didn't happen easily any more, not since he'd tattooed around his tear ducts. 'This is a very high-stress situation,' he said. He tried to visualize himself as a responsible, humane father, taking his kids on a family road trip. 'And we have to try and love each other.'

'*Thank* you, Michael,' Elizabeth said, and for a couple of miles all was peaceful. Then Marlon started in again on the ring.

'So these Krupps. They make the weapons that knock off your people, by the millions – and then you buy up their baubles? How does that work?'

Elizabeth twisted around in the front seat until she could look Marlon in the eye.

'What *you* don't understand is that when Richard put this ring on my finger it stopped meaning *death* and started meaning *love*.'

'Oh, I see. You have the power to turn death into love, just like that.'

Elizabeth smiled discreetly at Michael. She squeezed his hand, and he squeezed hers back. '*Just like that*,' she whispered.

Marlon snorted. 'Well, good luck to you. But back in the real world a thing is what it is, and thinking don't make it otherwise.'

Elizabeth took a compact from a hidden fold of her stole and reapplied some very red lipstick. 'You know,' she told him, 'Andy once said it would be very glamorous to be reincarnated as my ring. That's an actual quotation.'

'Sounds about right,' Marlon said, spoiling the moment and sounding pretty sneery, which seemed, to Michael, more than a little unfair, for whatever you thought about Andy personally, as a person, surely if anybody had understood their mutual suffering, if anyone had predicted, prophet-like, the exact length and strength and connective angles and occasionally throttling power of their three-way love thread, it was Andy.

'"It is no gift I tender,"' Marlon read, very loudly. '"A loan is all I can; But do not scorn the lender; Man gets no more from Man."'

'This is *not* the time for poetry!' Elizabeth shouted.

'This is *exactly* the time for poetry!' Marlon shouted.

Just then, Michael remembered that there were a few CDs in the glove box. If he believed in anything, he believed in the healing power of music. He reached over to open it and passed the cases to Elizabeth.

'I honestly don't think we should stop in Ohio,' she said, examining them and then pushing a disc into the slit. 'We could take turns driving. We'll drive through the night.'

'I can't drive when I'm tired,' Marlon said, hitching himself up into a semi-upright position. 'Or hungry. Maybe I should do my shift now.'

'And I'll do the night shift,' Michael said, brightening, and he began looking for a place to stop. He could not get over how well he was handling the apocalypse so far. Sure, he was terrified, but, at the same time, oddly elated and – vitally – not especially medicated, for his assistant had all his stuff, and he hadn't told her he was escaping from New York until they were already on the road, fearing his assistant would try to stop him, as she usually tried to stop him doing the things he most wanted to do. Now he was beyond everyone's reach. He struggled to think of another moment in his life when he'd felt so free. Was that terrible to say? He had to confess to himself that he felt high, and now tried to identify the source. The adrenaline of self-survival? Mixed with the pity, mixed with the horror? He wondered: is this the feeling people have in war zones and the like? Or – another strange thought – was this in fact what civilian people generally feel every day of their lives, in their sad old rank-smelling Toyota Camrys, sitting in traffic on their way to their workplaces, or camping outside your hotel window, or fainting in front of your dancing image on the JumboTron? This feeling of no escape from your situation – of forced acceptance? Of no escape even from your escape?

'Marlon, did you know that when Liz and I, when we have sleepovers . . . ?' Michael said, a little too quickly, and aware that he was babbling, but unable to stop. 'Well, I really don't sleep at all! Not one wink. Unless you literally knock me out? I'm literally awake all night long. So I'm good to drive all the way to Brentwood. I mean, if we have to.'

'Don't stop till you get enough,' Marlon murmured, and lay back down.

'I dreamed a dream in time gone *byyyyyy*,' Liz sang, along with the CD, 'when hope was high and life worth *liviiiiiing*. I dreamed that love would never *diiiiie*! I prayed that God would be for-*giviiiiing*.'

It was the sixth or seventh go-round. They were almost in Harrisburg, having been considerably slowed by two stops at Burger King, one at McDonald's, and three separate visits to KFC.

'If you play that song one more time,' Marlon said, eating a bucket of wings, 'I'm going to kill you myself.'

The sun was setting on the deep-orange polyvinyl-chloride blinds in their booth, and Michael felt strongly that his new role as the Decider must also include some aspect of spiritual guidance. To that end, he passed Marlon the maple syrup and said, in his high-pitched but newly determined tones, 'You know, guys, we've driven six hours already and, well, we haven't talked at all about what happened back there.'

They were sitting in an IHOP, just the other side of the Appalachian Mountains, with their mirrored shades on, eating pancakes. Michael had decided – two fast-food joints and eighty miles ago – to leave his usual disguise in the trunk of the car. It had become obvious that it wasn't necessary, no, not today. And now, with an overwhelming feeling of liberation, he removed his shades, too. For as it was in KFC, in Burger King, and beneath the Golden Arches, so it was in this IHOP: every soul in the place was watching television. Even the waitress who served them watched the television while she served, and spilled a little hot coffee on Michael's glove, and didn't say sorry and didn't clean it up, nor did she notice that Marlon wasn't wearing shoes – or that he was Marlon – or that resting beside the salt shaker was a diamond as big as the Ritz.

'I feel like one minute we were in the Garden, and it was a dream,' Elizabeth said, slowly. 'And we were happy, we were celebrating this marvellous boy' – she squeezed Michael's hand – 'celebrating thirty years of your wonderful talent, my dear, and everything was just *beautiful*. And then –' She hugged her coffee mug with both hands and brought it to her lips. 'And then, well, "*the tigers came*" – and now it really feels like the end of days. I know that sounds silly, but that's how it feels to me. There's a childlike part of me that just wants to *rewind* twenty-four hours.'

'Make that twenty-four years,' Marlon snapped, but with his classic wry Marlon smile, and all you could do was forgive him. 'Scratch that,' he said, hamming it up now. 'Make it forty.'

Elizabeth pursed her lips and made an adorable comic face. She looked like Amy, in *Little Women*, doing some sly calculation in her head. 'Come to think of it,' she said, 'forty would work out just swell for me, too.'

'Not me,' Michael said, letting a lot of air out of his mouth in a great rush so that he would be brave enough to say what he wanted to say, whether or not it was appropriate, whether or not it was the normal kind of thing you said in abnormal times like these. But perhaps this was his only real advantage, in this moment, over every other person in the IHOP and most of America: nothing normal had ever happened to him, not ever, not in his whole conscious life. And so there was a little part of him that was always prepared for the monstrous, familiar with it, and familiar, too, with its necessary counterbalancing force: love. He reached across the table and took the hands of his two dear friends in his own.

'I don't want to be in any other moment than this one,' he told them. 'Here. With you two. No matter how awful it gets. I want to be with you and with all these people. With everyone on earth. In this moment.'

They were all silent for a second, and then Marlon raised his still-gorgeous eyebrows, sighed, and said, 'Hate to break it to you, buddy, but you don't have much choice about it either way. Looks like no one's gonna beam us up. Whatever this shit is –' he gestured toward the air in front of them, to the molecules within the air, to time itself – 'we're stuck in it, just like everybody.'

'Yes,' Michael said. He was smiling, and it was the presence of a smile – unprecedented in that IHOP, on that day – that, more than anything else, finally attracted the waitress's attention. 'Yes,' he said. 'I know.'

Big Week

I

He sat in the dive bar on Sherman, looking out at his house, on the other side of the street. The panels were buckled along the porch, and deep, ugly breaches scored the white clapboard – they had sort of an agonized look about them. But come spring – if spring ever came – he would fix it all up for her, repaint and re-seal, whatever needed doing. That went for the oil tank, too. He would carry on doing whatever was necessary around the place, because he loved her and saw nothing but good in her, and she still loved him – in the largest sense of that word – and people would just have to wrap their heads around that fact.

'But how's it *work* exactly?' asked a Mr Frank Everett, whose one-room bar it was. He came out from behind the counter, and joined his only customer at the window. 'Not your house any more, is it?'

He was looking straight past Everett, off into some noble horizon, though when Everett followed his gaze all he saw was a rack of Twinkies sweating in the window of the gas station.

'That's correct,' he told Everett, 'I'm giving it to her. She deserves it. And anything she needs doing, I'll do it for her, she only has to ask. I'm happy to do it. I want her to be happy.'

Everett lifted a half-full glass and put a cardboard coaster beneath it.

'See, that's the bit I don't get. You still go to church with her. She makes you cookies.'

'She makes me cookies.'

The manager folded his arms and took on a look of priestly awe, as if Marie's cookies were truly the Alpha and Omega. He was not Irish, Frank, nor even from Boston, but had once been married to the type and felt he understood his customers; their tastes and habits, their humour.

'Got to the point with my Annette,' he confessed, covering his eyes with a dishrag, 'and I don't mind telling you – got to the point wherein I was gonna hire someone to kill her. No word of a lie.' He measured a tiny gap with the fingers of his free hand: 'I was this close.'

He whipped the rag aside and laughed amiably, but the man – whose name was Michael Kennedy McRae – sat unsmiling and reproachful, like a puppy thwacked on the nose with a rolled-up *Herald*.

'Well,' McRae said, flushing a little, 'I'd have to say it's not that way for us. We've cried and we've held each other. A lot of people round here may think of me different these days . . . She never did.'

Went back to staring nobly out the window. There seemed no way to tell him that his face was green, the consequence of a pair of fluorescent shamrocks attached to the glass.

'McRae – you're unusual,' said Frank, patting him on the back, though he did not find him unusual in any particular. There were five McRae siblings and they were all of them talkers. And they all looked like Donald O'Connor, more or less – even the women.

'Want another?' asked Frank, after a minute, and got no reply. 'Hey, McRae, You're not sore over that little Annette joke are you? That's stupid.'

Yet it was true enough he would not have dared make such a gag in front of McRae a few months ago. Wouldn't have joked about as much as a parking ticket.

'McRae?'

Half-standing on his stool, big square head craned urgently leftwards. An old bull, rising up from its knees. Everett could see the outline of tensed muscles from here, even through slacks. Primed! People don't change. They could fire McRae ten more times – he'd always be a cop.

'Sorry, Frank, you must want to get home. Should have said – I'm waiting for my boy. Thought that was his car. It won't be much longer. He's probably just caught behind a gritter somewhere. He's coming from the art school.'

Frank looked up and worked a dishcloth round the inside of a quart glass.

'Makes no difference to me. I don't close for snow and I don't close for empty. I don't close.'

'With three boys, everybody said – well, you know, all the usual warnings. But he's in the middle – natural born peacemaker. Marie's idea is he's the gentlest of all of them. God bless him. We're so proud of him. I mean, we worry, too. I shouldn't have said art school – it's the Art Institute. Different place. Not painting – "graphic arts". That worries her, a little. I don't know.'

'Plenty of call for graphics. Everything's made out of graphics.'

'We'll see.'

Fifteen minutes later a tall young man in a Red Sox cap parked his mother's car outside the family home and trudged through the snow in unsuitable shoes. He was a head and shoulders lankier than his father, skinnier, too, and his face, though good-natured and open, did not have Mike's sharp architecture. He shook the powder from his feet and smiled bemusedly as his father met him at the threshold of the bar, hugged the boy tightly round his middle, and burst into unabashed tears.

'Hey, Dad . . . Hey, it's all right. Let's sit. You're getting yourself all worked up.'

The son manoeuvred them inside into the warm. The look of ardent love in the father's eyes was such that even Frank, ten yards away, felt oppressed by it.

'Oh, boy, look at that: cried on you,' said McRae, poking at the wet patches on his son's shirt, while the young man gazed calmly down at his father's finger, waiting for him to finish. Something about this scene put Frank in mind of St Thomas, up to the knuckle in stigmata. But of course that was the kid's name: Tommy.

'Boy oh boy, I'm sorry . . . And the thing that's nuts is I'm not even sad! I'm so grateful and blessed right now! Look at me! I'm the luckiest man in the world.'

'Okay, Dad. Let's sit, though. Let's just sit right here.'

Gently the younger McRae pried the elder's hands off his person, held them for a moment between his own, then placed them gently on the table.

'Sorry I'm late. You look well, Dad.'

'Nah, I'm ten pounds over. Fifteen. I can't run – so. All I know is running and cycling. And the doctor's put the nix on both. I gotta figure out what I can do now! Driving's got me sitting down all day.' McRae reached over and played a strange sort of jig on his son's knees. 'Hey, you going over to your mother's after?'

'Um . . . Sure.'

'Good, that's good.'

Frank came over with a pair of Guinnesses, on a tray no less.

'Your old man instructed me,' he said, and set the sloping drinks down. 'He was real clear: when the kid comes, bring out the black stuff, it's his favourite.'

'Great,' said the son, but took only the vaguest sip of froth, without any sign of pleasure. Mike left his exactly where it was.

'I mean, look at this kid. The length of his arms! They tried to hustle him into basketball – well, of course they would – but no interest, none whatsoever. He's his mother's child. She plays the piano, loves pictures. He's a musical, visual person.'

The son sighed, pointed a finger at his own temple and pulled the trigger: 'Arty.'

'Hey, it's a great thing! Don't despise it! Not everybody can like sports. Be a dull world if they did.' Mike batted at the peak of the baseball cap. 'What *is* that, anyway? Late-life conversion?'

'Kim's.'

'His girl's Korean,' explained McRae. 'And I really couldn't be happier.'

'Nice,' said Frank.

'Couldn't be happier. Marie either. We're so proud for both of them. Kim's at the art school, too. Art is a wonderful thing.

Education – that's another wonderful thing. It's a gift. But it's not free! I've put three boys through college now and I'm telling you: it's not easy. Guys like us, we never got that far, never expected to – but even if we had, who would've paid for it? It's serious money!'

Frank whistled: 'And it's the middle-class that's getting squeezed!'

'Right. But we're in it together, me and Marie – together but apart – if you see what I mean. Bottom line: we've always sacrificed for these children. Only place we ever been as a family is Hawaii. Twice. Never been to Europe. Never been to Ireland. But Michael Junior went to France – all over France, for a whole summer. Joe went to Spain that time. And Tommy – you went somewhere with Father Torday – years ago –'.

'Edinborough.'

'Right, Edinborough!' McRae reached out and squeezed his son's shoulder. 'And I feel I went to these places, through my boys. And that's what I'm talking about. If you love your children you make these sacrifices – they're not even sacrifices, they're just what you do. And all of that – it can't just end because it's over! We're a family. Twenty-nine happy years – happiest of my life. Honestly, meeting your mother was the luckiest thing that ever happened to me. I stand by that, Tom, I really do.'

'Okay, Dad,' murmured Tommy, but looked grateful, a moment later, for the interruption of a sudden stream of cold air through the door, along with two men in blue, from National Grid. 'Maybe we should let Frank get on and run his bar.'

'I am truly a blessed man. I tell that to everyone.'

'Born optimist,' Frank confirmed, though in his own mind

the correct noun was slightly longer. 'Now, can I get you guys anything else? All good? Okay, then.'

As Frank walked away, McRae shunted his stool still closer to his son until their knees touched.

'Wow, is your mom gonna be so pleased to see you. She saw Joe last week but she hasn't seen MJ since Christmas. Well, just think of me, when you're eating that leg of lamb – I'll be right under your feet.'

The boy pulled off his baseball cap: 'You're – you're not eating with us?'

'No, Tom, not tonight. We've got to start making this official, haven't we, at some point? I've been the troll under the bridge for . . . well, a year almost. And your mother's still a beautiful woman; I mean, *I* still find her beautiful, *I* still find her sexy – and the fact is she'll get online soon enough, and then there'll be a whole lot of billy goats, you know, wanting to come trip-trapping over –'

'Oh, Dad . . .'

'Hey, I'm happy for her! I don't even *want* to drink –' he pushed the Guinness aside; it slid disconcertingly along the table, stopping just shy of the edge – 'Don't know why I even ordered that. Tom, I gotta tell you: right now I feel like life is just this *precious* . . . this very *precious* – I don't even know what, I don't actually have the right word ready for you right now – but I can tell you I feel it's precious. And I just want to feel everything that there is to feel, good or bad, and I've realized that I don't need . . . Hey – you wanna eat? Food's good here. Oh, right, right – you're eating over there, I forgot. That's good. Come here.'

Tom McRae submitted to a benign headlock. His adult self,

his city self – who only this morning had been confidently discussing the genius of Cindy Sherman with the adult children of lawyers and doctors – now shrank and slipped away, to be replaced by an earlier incarnation: the shy, suburban, middle son, hiding his eyes behind hair.

'It just feels weird,' he said and took hold of his drink with both hands, lifting it to his lips like a milkshake. 'I mean, not that I want you guys to get all dramatic, but – it's weirdly peaceful, that's all.'

'Oh, it's the peace-fullest divorce in history!' cried McRae. 'That's what I was just saying to Frank! Never even hollered at each other in almost thirty years.'

'Right. That's how I remember it. But Kim – she's like: no way dude, must be false memory syndrome. But I was like: no, I remember how it was. But, look, we – we don't have to talk about any of this.'

'Oh, no, no – Tom, I don't mind talking about it. I like talking about it. Actually, it's good for me. I talk about it all the time. I have this rule – and I'm not trying to God-bother you Tommy, I've never done that, you know that – but the fact is, this is how I'm thinking now; I say to myself: would you, Mike McRae, say this that or the other if Jesus Christ himself was at your shoulder? And if I wouldn't then I don't. Simple as that.'

McRae reached forward and wiped a foam moustache from his son's frowning face.

'Me and your mother were having this very beautiful conversation a few weeks back – she'd come downstairs to give me back this Japanese breadknife I gave her to slice some beef she got from that little place on – that's not important – the point is, we're having this conversation, very forgiving, very honest, and she says: "I wanna travel, I wanna meet new people, I wanna get back to my music, to playing the piano like I used to. Thirty years ago I settled for Mike McRae, and now I'm fifty-six and I don't want to settle any more." Oof. Right in the solar plexus. Now, Tom, that was a hard thing to hear. It was. But, if that's how a person feels, that's how they feel. We got three beautiful boys. I can honestly stand here and say: I haven't a single regret. Not one. I was lucky to meet her. So lucky.'

'Well, that's great, Dad,' said Tommy – he could not seem to stop dabbing anxiously at his own philtrum with a napkin – 'just as long as you're – you know, just as long as you're in a good place, I guess.'

'I'm in a *great* place.' McRae opened his startling blue eyes about as wide as they'd go. 'Let me ask you something: you ever see *The Sound of Music*?'

'Sure.'

'"*When God closes a door he opens a window*."'

Tommy tried valiantly to smile.

'That's like a line from that movie. That really kills me! So, what I'm saying is, I got a few things on the burner – I don't wanna talk about them right now – I know I'm talking your ear off – but suffice to say I think you're going to approve, Tommy, I really do. I mean, most of it you know already. So today's Sunday – Monday, Tuesday: I'm working. Fine. Wednesday I'm going to the library – see if I can still at least be a Friend of the Library. Look, I know they can't put me on the action committee any more, not in any official way – of course I understand that. But no harm in asking, right?'

'No harm.'

'And Friday – Friday I move out – that's it. That's the day.'

'Big week.'

'Big week.'

A buzz came from Mike McRae's waistband. His son smiled tenderly at the sight of his father retrieving some wire-framed reading glasses from the top pocket of his sports jacket and perusing the tiny screen with as much attentive care as some quaint old kook in a Rockwell painting, reading the baseball scores.

'Only guy I know who still owns a beeper.'

McRae looked up over his half-moons with a wide-open, undimmed enthusiasm that made even his gentlest son fear for him.

'Really? A lot of the guys at work have 'em.'

2

The name on the card was Clark: they were to meet in the ten-minute waiting zone just outside Departures. But Clark was late and the morning frigid. McRae got back in his car, drove around, parked in the lot and walked into Baggage Claim. He checked his beeper, held up his card. All the other guys wore suits, had iPad screens instead of cardboard, and their passengers came sooner: a series of middle-aged executives glued to their devices, handing over their bags and asking fearfully about the weather. But now an elegant lady appeared at the top of an escalator, and waved at Mike McRae; a tall lady, slender and dark, with black silky hair and a very red mouth, who looked like she could run a 5K without pausing for breath.

'Clark?'

'Urvashi Clark.'

'Perfect. You got any bags?'

She did, but insisted on carrying them. They made their way through a sideways snow-flurry to an elevator and then up to a luxury sedan on the second floor. Everything she wore was black; black-framed glasses, black overcoat and, around her neck, a black fur which she placed beside her on the back seat where its fine hairs quivered like a nervous animal.

'Looks like we're going to the university.'

'Please.'

She took out a thin folder, the exact shade of her lipstick, opened it and began shuffling papers around.

'You giving a lecture?'

'A paper,' she said, without lifting her eyes from her folder. 'It's a conference on architecture. I'm an architect.'

He let her be. Drove through the complex of flyovers, entered a shaded tunnel.

'Need light?'

But by the time he'd thought to ask they were emerging out the other side, into light so white, so penetrating, it seemed to erase all distinctions – not least the one dividing the front of the car from the back – and Mike McRae felt he could no longer reasonably pretend he was not in a small, shared space with a beautiful woman in the full glory of the day.

'Architecture. Must be interesting.'

'Hmmm.'

'Gothic architecture, modern architecture. I guess I'm a traditionalist. I like a white picket fence. I like a stained-glass window. Of course, in Boston we got a lot of beautiful old buildings.'

'Certainly have.'

'A lot,' said Mike emphatically, though at that moment they happened to be passing a 7-Eleven encased in a huge grey box. 'That what your paper's about?'

'Mine? No.' She withdrew an iPhone from her back pocket and held it in front of her like a shield, but it gave Mike an opportunity to glimpse her left hand, and this was an aspect of his new life that did not yet come naturally: he had to remind himself each time. Nor was he always sure of the correct interpretation. A single black stone in twisted gold, on the second finger.

'Not annoying you by asking, am I?'

'Not at all,' said Urvashi, meeting the expectant blue eyes in the rear-view. 'Well, I suppose it's about . . . well, how certain spaces determine – shape – our lives.'

McRae slapped the steering wheel: 'Now, that just rings so true to me. So true! Because, I'm from Charlestown – three generations. And Charlestown shaped me, and my family, absolutely. Absolutely.'

'Ah, how interesting.' She leaned forward. 'In what way?'

'Oh, values, principles, beliefs. There's just a Charlestown way of looking at things, I guess.'

'I see,' she said, sat back and returned to her phone.

'Yeah,' said Mike, a few minutes later, as if no time had passed. 'Ten years ago, we moved to Cambridge, for our sins, but really everything important that ever happened to me in my life happened in Charlestown. Met my wife walking through the rain in Charlestown – not on the street, I mean – she lived there. We had a friend in common – I needed a place to stay for the night, and I didn't want to bother my mother – she had enough on her plate. And I'm between apartments – cos this was when I was twenty-two years old, working as a courier, and somebody's just stolen my bike – anyway, point is, I have a canvas bag with this great wad of paper in it that I haven't delivered yet. Five-hundred-page document, a manuscript, important to the guy who wrote it, I'm thinking – and this is before the Internet! So this is the only copy. And I'm trudging through Charlestown looking for Marie's place; she was rooming with two other girls – and I'm getting soaked! So finally I get there and there she is, with ice skates over her shoulder, on her way out – and she says: "Make yourself at home." Holding these ice skates, looking back over her shoulder at me. Beautiful then and she's beautiful now. So I make myself at home. I look at my bag and I'm like: Oh, man, I'm in trouble. I laid out each piece of paper to dry. Five-hundred-some pages laid out on every surface of her apartment, on the doors, on the bed, off the ironing board, everywhere! She came home, didn't even blink. "Make yourself at home." Boy, did she ever mean that. I stayed that night, the next night – thirty years we spent together. Of course, we're separating now.'

'Oh – I'm sorry.'

'Don't be! Look at me. I'm the luckiest man you'll ever meet.'

To prove it he lifted a little in his seat until the mirror accepted the full toothy brilliance of his smile.

'Bottom line? This is a transitional period for me. I'm driving a car part-time, as you can see. I got an injury running – then I had this operation. Couldn't work for a while, couldn't run.'

'That must be frustrating.'

Urvashi picked up one of the little bottles of water from the drinks holder, took a large swig and, then, a little risk: 'I run. Not very far, but I like to do it.'

Mike slapped the steering wheel again: 'Knew you did! Knew you were a runner just by looking at you!'

'Oh, I don't know that I'd call myself a runner exactly. I never get beyond three miles.'

'Question of will,' McRae said, holding up two fingers. 'Believe me, I know. I've run Ironmans, half marathons, whole marathons . . .'

She gave a little shudder and looked out the window.

'No, I could never do that. I don't have . . . whatever that is.'

'Nah, everybody has it. You wanna know the secret? You do it for that feeling you get in the last minute. That's what you're looking for. Look, our lives are easy, right? We switch a button; the light comes on. Press another button, food gets cooked. But you gotta dig deeper than that when you run – into some deeper part of you. That part exists in everyone. Just a matter of finding it again. All be a lot happier if we did.'

'I'm sure you're right. I may be too old to start, however.'

'Hey, you're not as old as me. I'm fifty-seven! Ran my first marathon at forty-two. Ran it when I was fifty-three, fifty-four and fifty-six. Up until this injury. Then they prescribe me Oxy-Contin. Well, of *course* I get addicted to Percocet. Which leads to heroin. I mean, heroin's cheaper! Isn't that crazy? That *heroin* is cheaper? Well, all of that got me into a lot of situations. A lot of situations. And the scary thing is, I wasn't even in that much pain. You know? Like maybe I should have just experienced the pain.'

They stopped at a traffic light. He twisted right round in his seat to further discuss the problem of pain, and in the same moment some act of grace made her phone buzz, and buzz again. Mike looked concernedly at the device.

'Could be important. You'd better take that.'

Grateful, she picked up the beloved thing, and with a face that suggested the intense business of work or love, commenced scrolling idly through her junk mail.

'Truth is I lost myself,' murmured Mike McRae, 'lost myself completely.' He stopped sharply to allow a mother and baby to cross the street. 'Now, people ask me what I mean by that. Well, let me give you just one example from literally thousands.' He checked the rear-view. 'I'll wait till you're done with that.'

Urvashi placed her phone face down on the seat.

'So I'm going across the park – in deep snow – to pick my youngest son up from this rapping concert –' He took a short, deep breath and winced: 'Ah, this is hard talking.'

'Oh, but you really don't have to –'

'Very low moment in my life. So, he's gone to see some kind of a rapper – I'm blanking on his name. Real famous, this guy.'

Urvashi threw out the names she knew, doing her best to describe each man physically. For a while it seemed like she would be doing this for the rest of her life.

'You know what? Now I think about it, I believe this person was a white gentleman.'

And in this far smaller pond, it proved to be the second fish.

'Right! But with my new addict brain all I'm thinking is: I'll call my guy, get the stuff halfway across the park, then I'll have time to smoke, then go meet my boy. Perfect! That's addict logic right there. So that's what I do. And I'm floating, right? In my mind. But actually I'm lying in three feet of snow, and if this dog hadn't wandered over and licked my face, I probably would have died out there, of hypothermia or what-have-you. So now at least I'm awake and somehow I make it across this field to the lot where the stadium is. And I see all these kids, and they're all fired up – like they're really *in* life. And my Joe is the same way. Fired up! The look on his face! Now, frankly, I don't approve of that type of music – isn't music at all, I don't believe – but I'm standing there thinking, wait a minute: this is what JC did, right? Got 'em all fired up. My kid's all fired up – and here I am like a zombie. I'm like the walking dead. Man, that was a low moment.'

'I – I – imagine.'

She looked up finally from her lap; she sensed water running alongside the car, racing to keep up. With her fur she wiped the condensation from the window. Boathouse. Geese. Young men in red, heaving oars, blowing clouds from their mouths.

'I can't imagine being on the water on a day like this,' she said, brightly as possible, for they seemed to have entered a conversational wilderness. Where were the breadcrumbs that led back to small talk?

'All about will. I really prided myself on my will. Had a little too much pride in it, probably. Then I lost it all.' He twisted right round in his seat again. 'Miss Clark, mind if I ask where you're from?'

'Not at all. Uganda.'

When he frowned two deep ridges appeared in his forehead. Urvashi resisted the urge to put a finger between them.

'See now, I would have said Pakistan or India or Bangladesh or even Iraq or Iran, maybe. I would not have said Uganda.'

'Well, there used to be a big South Asian population in Uganda.'

'Oh!' He turned back to the wheel. 'And . . . can I ask how old are you?'

'I'm forty-six.'

'Wow, wouldn't have guessed that either. Can I say you look a lot younger?'

'Please do. Only Americans get offended by compliments.'

'And your husband, kids – they here in Boston?'

She smiled at the sweet simplicity of the attempt.

'My partner and I live in New York. I don't have any children.'

His face fell and she felt suddenly very sorry, for she had presented him with the inconceivable. But it would take too long and be altogether too laborious to put his mind at rest; to make clear all the many ways in which she was happy, how she loved her work, her lover, her freedom. Instead, on a whim, she conjured up two non-existent stepchildren, girls, in their teens.

'Ah, so you know the drill,' said Mike McRae, grinning conspiratorially. 'So let me tell you something that'll blow your mind. I got three sons, right? Boston Irish as the day is long. But my oldest boy's wife is African-American, from Chicago, so his daughter is kinda like your colour – and my middle son's girlfriend is Korean! Now, the youngest is not seeing anybody at the moment, but I'm thinking, what's next? Chinese? Right? Or maybe the next'll be an Ind– Native American. Maybe the next'll be Native American! Point is: we're all God's children. Me and my wife – we're separating – but we're thrilled. When I first saw my little brown granddaughter –' his eyes teared up as he took a hand off the wheel and placed it on his breastbone – 'it was like my heart got larger and there was a new room in it. A new chamber.'

To this, his beautiful passenger said nothing at all; only bit her blood-red lip and looked out the window. He could not know that her mind had drifted strangely: to her imagined stepdaughters, whom she placed now in rooms of her own design – twin eyries either side of a chimney breast – in a shingled house that sat on a bluff, over a wild beach of dunes and sea grass, in America or in Africa – in some dream combination of the two. Mike, believing he had caused offence, stood the silence for as long as he could. He turned on the radio. Put the wipers on. Spied a meth-faced girl leaving a pharmacy with something stuffed down the back of her pants. The shadow life. He saw it everywhere – it was a kind of second sight – but what use was it? He took a left towards campus. He looked back at his passenger, her face anxious, turned away. Her window misted, a single cloud. What could she possibly see?

3.

It had cost six million dollars and was described as a 're-imagining' but to Mike it looked like someone had taken a large box of concrete and glass, put wheels under it and driven it into the side of the old library. On the other hand, it seemed busier than he remembered it, with somebody at every one of the new terminals, and many more waiting to use them. A lot of homeless folks, easily spotted by their shoes: elaborate self-creations, or else combinations of several pairs, wound together with duct-tape. A uniform had once allowed him to speak to such people; now he stood, undifferentiated and unnoticed among them, waiting in the 'atrium' for a Miss Wendy English, the senior administrator. There were so many possible entrances and exits to the new space he didn't know from which to expect her, and in the end it was an ambush: the feel of a little finger poking him in the back.

'Miss Wendy. Now look at you. Wowee. Did you get younger?'

'I had my seventy-fifth birthday last week and I've decided to stop right there. It's good to see you, Michael.'

They clasped hands, which required, from McRae, a certain delicacy. She was five foot one, weighed only about eighty pounds in her skirt-suit, and he could feel each vein and bone.

'Long time,' she said. They stepped back and admired each other. Six months. Evidently she had stopped dyeing her hair; the small, stately afro white as lambswool.

'Really appreciative of you seeing me today,' he said, and for a ridiculous moment feared he was about to weep. 'Means a lot.'

'Means nothing at all,' she said, gesturing at the high, light space. 'As you can see, we're open to everybody. And I meant what I said: it's good to see you. Let's go to my office.'

But she walked quickly, always slightly ahead, and of the many people who stopped to salute Miss Wendy or ask her some practical question – in the atrium, through the corridors – not one of them did she introduce to Mike McRae. By the time they reached her corner office, back in the old red-brick building, he felt like a pale shadow, chasing this little dark woman through the world.

'Now, what can I do for you, Michael?'

She sat behind her gigantic walnut desk, bird-arms folded on the green baize, and McRae thought of Alice McRae – mother of six, admirer of Louise Day Hicks – for whom this image of her son, cap in hand before a tiny old black lady, would have been incomprehensible.

'Michael – you okay?'

'Oh, I'm *great*.' He put his fingers to both eyes as a deterrent. 'You know, when the whole community comes around you like people have, well, that just feels great. And after all the stuff in the papers there was a lot of support – a lot of love.'

'You are a part of this community,' she said, looking directly into his eyes, as few people did these days, and separating each word like she was counting pearls on a necklace. But when she got to the end of the rope, there was nothing further.

'Right,' said McRae, into the gap, 'and I feel I've got a lot more to give, to this library in particular. That veterans programme we spoke about last year – I would love to help implement that. I feel like a lot of the skills I have – plus the skills I've been acquiring recently, because I should explain – look, I haven't even told my own family this, but that's the effect you have on me, I guess –' He laughed, a little wildly. 'Those eyes, Miss Wendy. You got a bit of witchcraft in those eyes – truth serum! What I was going to say is I've acquired a lot of new skills in this programme I've been in these past few months – and, well, the big reveal is I'm actually training to become a substance-abuse counsellor. Yep. So this is a big week for me, I qualify this week – and I really feel that twenty-five years as an officer, plus my own personal experience with substance-abuse issues, and now this training – I really feel I could have a whole new role on the action committee here, a really substantial role, that would bring a lot of added value.'

Throughout this speech Miss Wendy remained perfectly

still. Behind her, snow fell steadily. She looked like a tiny frowning saint, carved into the ebony of an apse.

'I can't put you back on the committee, Mike. I'm sorry.'

Down came the snow. Silent, thick. He leaned forward and gripped the desk.

'How much money did I raise for this library? I must have run two hundred miles for this library, Miss Wendy. Two hundred miles.'

'At least. But you were treasurer, Michael, and I suppose – in the light of recent events – the board feels . . .'

She carried on talking. He looked past her, to the snow, and saw a paltry thirty bucks folded in a wallet – property of some street kid in the cells – and saw this same thirty in his own pocket, and tried now to separate his physical memory of these images from the CCTV, unsure any more if he had any real memory distinct from the footage. Thirty bucks. The more he watched it at the tribunal the more random and disconnected it had seemed. What did it have to do with the real life of Michael Kennedy McRae? Why should that misbegotten moment – from so far back in the story, back when it was still just a matter of ten or twelve pills a day – why should that turn out to be the definitive act? You could drive yourself crazy wondering about a thing like that. And then there were other days when he was able, for a moment, to be objective, and see there was no mystery to it, no special fate or particular curse. It was only what he and his colleagues had often casually referred to as the Capone Effect. When you get done, you rarely get done for the right thing.

'– all of which puts me,' Miss Wendy was saying, 'in a very difficult position. The drugs we could get over. But the money . . .' She spread her hands in a gesture of helplessness. McRae rose to his feet.

'When I was a cop – and I was a good cop for a long time – I operated with discretion. Always. That's the most important part of the job. Knowing when to come down hard and when to go easy. Miss Wendy, I'm asking you to exercise your discretion. I'm begging you, actually.'

She sighed and looked away.

'You're asking me for a thing I cannot do.' She stood up. Snow. 'Mike, you and me go back a long way. And I know you're one of the good guys,' she began, 'but it's simply –' She had run out of pearls.

'Am I?' he asked.

4

'Mike? That you?'

He had one of the last boxes in his arms, filled with the random, unclassifiable stuff that didn't seem to go anywhere else. He had hoped to finish before she got home.

When she saw him, she put a hand on the flat part of her chest: 'You scared me.'

'SWAT-team feet,' he said, as he had said so many times before. 'Silent and deadly.'

She was holding a grey-blue book of music, Bach's something or other.

'It's fine,' she said, 'but Mrs Akinson'll be here any minute.'

'Mrs Akinson!' said Mike, with a face of marvel. 'That old

coot? Must have been sixty when she taught the boys. Gotta be at least ninety now.'

'Oh, she's not that old. Just has an old way of dressing.'

She walked forward and looked in his box and drew out a shoehorn shaped like Homer Simpson. She smiled sadly and put it back.

'Marie, you leave the door open again?'

She denied it. But a moment later came the sound of Mrs Akinson walking overhead, then a scale being played in a minor key.

Mike shrugged: 'SWAT-team ears.'

'Aren't you glad not to be doing that any more?'

'It was a part of the job.'

'Well aren't you glad it's not a part of *your* job?'

'Somebody's got to do it.'

'Maybe,' she said, and turned to go back upstairs.

'I got a new thing now,' he called after her and she sighed and stopped. 'It's been kind of a big week for me. I got this new gig, as a counsellor – substance abuse.'

Marie could think of a lot of things to say to that but she wanted to get to her piano lesson.

'That's great, Mike. I'm happy for you.'

'Oh, I'm really excited. It's a whole new direction for me. It's like a practical thing I can do with this feeling I got inside me. I've had it a long time – I guess I should have listened to it earlier. Would've saved us all a lot of pain. I think really it was when I got into my thirties, you know, that I just began to see that God is in other people, and he's in me. I can't explain it any better than that.'

Marie looked at McRae, the familiar welling water in his eyes. She looked right at him. She thought of the various time signatures of her life, as they had played out with this sentimental man, and it seemed to her a piece of music in which they themselves had been the notes. A steady trot at the start, turning so slow in that first year of marriage, when she had confessed to herself the lack of physical attraction. After that, things had gotten so fast – horribly, joyfully fast, almost ungraspable – for there was no way of slowing the children, nor the years of her life they held tight in their sweaty little fists. All the irretrievable hours spent in cars with sticks and balls, ferrying them here and there, cheering them on frozen sports fields, watching them, watching your own breath, walking their dogs, burying their dogs, shovelling the snow out of the drive, and then, a moment later, watching three tall young men, far taller than her – all with their father's eyes – shovelling snow out of the drive as a courtesy to their ageing mother. Sometimes they found a dog turd in that snow, or a pack of cigarettes, or somebody's ball – but never Marie as a girl. No. Nobody knew where that girl had gone. Fast! But slowing down again – almost stopping – the year they removed the breast. Slow like you move underwater, wondering if you'll surface again. Then she blinked three times and there were no more jockey shorts on the stairs, no filthy cereal bowls, no used condoms poorly hidden in an empty tube of Pringles, no brushes rigid with dried paint, no rackets and no balls. She loved her grandchildren, and the alien world they brought with them, but her daughter-in-law was one of these women who act like babies start the whole concerto up once more, from the top. A lovely idea, but not true, not for Marie. They were not her babies. Nor had an empty house made her sad, as she had been warned it would. Instead, time began to cautiously reshape itself round her broken body, and she found she wanted to be alone with it once more. That's just how she felt – and she would have felt that way even if Mike had been clean as the Pope and retired with full honours. In a strange way, he'd made everything easier. And now slowness beckoned again – if she stayed firm, if she managed to withstand that desperate look in the eyes of Michael Kennedy McRae. And what then? First things first. She'd lie down in the springtime grass, ask herself what just happened, looking down at her own body, distinct at last from every other body in the world.

Meet the President!

'What you got there, then?'

The boy didn't hear the question. He stood at the end of a ruined pier, believing himself quite alone. But now he registered the presence at his back, and turned.

'What you got there?'

A very old person, a woman, stood before him, gripping the narrow shoulder of a girl child. Both of them local, typically stunted, dim: they stared up at him stupidly. The boy turned again to the sea. All week long he had been hoping for a clear day to try out the new technology – not new to the world, but new to the boy – and now at last here was a break in the rain. Grey sky met grey sea. Not ideal, but sufficient. Ideally he would be standing on a cairn in Scotland or some other tropical spot, experiencing backlit clarity. Ideally he would be –

'Is it one of them what you see through?'

A hand, lousy with blue veins, reached out for the light encircling the boy's head, as if it were a substantial thing, to be grasped like the handle of a mug.

'Ooh, look at the green, Aggie. That shows you it's on.'

The boy was ready to play. He touched the node on his finger to the node at his temple, raising the volume.

'Course, he'd have to be somebody, Aggs, cos they don't

give 'em to nobody' – the boy felt the shocking touch of a hand on his own flesh. 'Are you somebody, then?'

She had shuffled around until she stood square in front of him, unavoidable. Hair as white as paper. A long, shapeless black dress, made of some kind of cloth, and what appeared to be a pair of actual glasses. Forty-nine years old, type O, a likelihood of ovarian cancer, some ancient debt infraction – nothing more. A blank, more or less. Same went for the girl: never left the country, eighty-five-per-cent chance of macular degeneration, an uncle on the database, long ago located, eliminated. She would be nine in two days. Melinda Durham and Agatha Hanwell. They shared no more DNA than strangers.

'Can you see us?' The old woman let go of her charge and waved her hands wildly. The tips of her fingers barely reached the top of the boy's head. 'Are we in it? What are we?'

The boy, unused to proximity, took a single step forward. Further he could not go. Beyond was the ocean; above, a mess of weather, clouds closing in on blue wherever blue tried to assert itself. A dozen or so craft darted up and down, diving low like seabirds after a fish, and no bigger than seabirds, skimming the dirty foam, then returning to the heavens, directed by unseen hands. On his first day here the boy had trailed his father on an inspection tour to meet those hands: intent young men at their monitors, over whose shoulders the boy's father leaned, as he sometimes leaned over the boy to ensure he ate breakfast.

'What d'you call one of them there?'

The boy tucked his shirt in all round: 'AG 12.'

The old woman snorted as a mark of satisfaction, but did not leave.

He tried looking the females directly in their dull brown eyes. It was what his mother would have done, a kindly woman with a great mass of waist-length flame-coloured hair, famed for her patience with locals. But his mother was long dead, he had never known her, he was losing what little light the day afforded. He blinked twice, said, 'Hand to hand.' Then, having a change of heart: 'Weaponry.' He looked down at his torso, to which he now attached a quantity of guns.

'You carry on, lad,' the old woman said. 'We won't get in your way. He can see it all, duck,' she told the girl, who paid her no mind. 'Got something in his hands – or thinks he does.'

She took a packet of tobacco from a deep pocket in the front of her garment and began to roll a cigarette, using the girl as a shield from the wind.

'Them clouds, dark as bulls. Racing, racing. They always win.' To illustrate, she tried turning Aggie's eyes to the sky, lifting the child's chin with a finger, but the girl would only gawk stubbornly at the woman's elbow. 'They'll dump on us before we even get there. If you didn't have to, I wouldn't go, Aggie, no chance, not in this. It's for you I do it. I've been wet and wet and wet. All my life. And I bet he's looking at blazing suns and people in their what-have-yous and altogethers! Int yer? Course you are! And who'd blame you?' She laughed so loud the boy heard her. And then the child – who did not laugh, whose pale face, with its triangle chin and enormous, fair-lashed eyes, seemed capable only of astonishment – pulled at his actual leg, forcing him to mute for a moment and listen to her question.

'Well, I'm Bill Peek,' he replied, and felt very silly, like somebody in an old movie.

'Bill Peek!' the old woman cried. 'Oh, but we've had Peeks

in Anglia a long time. You'll find a Peek or two or three down in Sutton Hoo. Bill Peek! You from round here, Bill Peek?'

His grandparents? Very possibly. Local and English – or his great-grandparents. His hair and eyes and skin and name suggested it. But it was not a topic likely to engage his father, and the boy himself had never felt any need or desire to pursue it. He was simply global, accompanying his father on his inspections, though usually to livelier spots than this. What a sodden dump it was! Just as everyone had warned him it would be. The only people left in England were the ones who couldn't leave.

'From round here, are you? Or maybe a Norfolk one? He looks like a Norfolk one, Aggs, wouldn't you say?'

Bill Peek raised his eyes to the encampment on the hill, pretending to follow with great interest those dozen circling, diving craft, as if he, uniquely, as the child of personnel, had nothing to fear from them. But the woman was occupied with her fag and the girl only sang 'Bill Peek, Bill Peek, Bill Peek' to herself, and smiled sadly at her own turned-in feet. They were too local even to understand the implied threat. He jumped off the pier onto the deserted beach. It was low tide – it seemed you could walk to Holland. He focused upon the thousands of tiny spirals on the sand, like miniature turds stretching out to the horizon.

Felixstowe, England. A Norman village; later, briefly, a resort, made popular by the German royal family; much fishing, once upon a time. A hundred years earlier, almost to the very month, a quaint flood had killed only forty-eight people. Over the years, the place had been serially flooded, mostly abandoned. Now the sad little town had retreated three miles inland and up a hill. Pop.: 850. The boy blinked twice more; he did not care much for history. He narrowed his attention to a single turd. *Arenicola marina*. Sandworms. Lugworms. These were its coiled castings. Castings? But here he found his interest fading once again. He touched his temple and said, 'Blood Head 4.' Then: 'Washington.' It was his first time at this level. Another world began to construct itself around Bill Peek, a shining city on a hill.

'Poor little thing,' Melinda Durham said. She sat on the pier, legs dangling, and pulled the girl into her lap. 'Demented with grief she is. We're going to a laying-out. Aggie's sister is laid out today. Her last and only relation. Course, the cold truth is, Aggie's sister weren't much better than trash, and a laying-out's a sight too good for her – she'd be better off laid out on this beach here and left for the gulls. But I ain't going for *her*. I do it for Aggie. Aggie knows why. Aggie's been a great help to me what with one thing and another.'

While he waited, as incidental music played, the boy idly checked a message from his father: at what time could he be expected back at the encampment? *At what time could he be expected*. This was a pleasing development, being an enquiry rather than an order. He would be fifteen in May, almost a man! A man who could let another man know when he could be expected, and let him know in his own sweet time, when he had the inclination. He performed some rudimentary stretches and bounced up and down on the balls of his feet.

'Maud, that was her name. And she was born under the same steeple she'll be buried under. Twelve years old. But so whorish –' Melinda covered Aggie's ears, and the girl leaned into the gesture, having mistaken it for affection. 'So whorish she looked like a crone. If you lived round here, Bill Peek, you'd've *known* Maud, if you understand me correctly. You would've known Maud right up to the biblical and beyond. Terrible. But Aggie's cut from quite different sod, thank goodness!' Aggie was released and patted on the head. 'And she's no one left, so here I am, muggins here, taking her to a laying-out when I've a million other stones to be lifted off the pile.'

The boy placed a number of grenades about his person. In each chapter of the Pathways Global Institute (in Paris, New York, Shanghai, Nairobi, Jerusalem, Tokyo), the boy had enjoyed debating with friends the question of whether it was better to augment around the 'facts on the ground', incorporating whatever was at hand ('flagging', it was called, the pleasure being the unpredictability), or to choose spots where there were barely any facts to work around. The boy was of the latter sensibility. He wanted to augment in clean, blank places, where he was free to fully extend, unhindered. He looked down the beach as the oil streaks in the sand were overlaid now with a gleaming pavement, lined on either side by the National Guard, saluting him. It was three miles to the White House. He picked out a large pair of breasts to wear, for reasons of his own, and a long, scaled tail, for purposes of strangulation.

'Oh, fuck a duck – you wouldn't do me an awful favour and keep an eye on Aggie just a minute, would you? – I've left my rosary! I can't go to no laying-out without it. It's more than my soul's worth. Oh, Aggie, how did you ever let me leave without it? She's a good girl, but she's thoughtless sometimes – her sister were thoughtless, too. Bill Peek, you will keep an eye on her, won't you? I won't be a moment. We're shacked up just on that hill by the old Martello tower. Eight minutes I'll be. No more. Would you do that for me, Bill Peek?'

Bill Peek nodded his head, once rightward, twice leftward. Knives shot out of his wrists and splayed beautifully like the fronds of a fern.

It was perhaps twenty minutes later, as he approached the pile of rubble – pounded by enemy craft – that had once been the Monument, that young Bill Peek felt again a presence at his back and turned and found Aggie Hanwell with her fist in her mouth, tears streaming, jaw working up and down in an agonized fashion. He couldn't hear her over the explosions. Reluctantly, he paused.

'She ain't come back.'

'Excuse me?'

'She went but she ain't come back!'

'Who?' he asked, but then scrolled back until he found it. 'M. Durham?'

The girl gave him that same astonished look.

'My Melly,' she said. 'She promised to take me but she went and she ain't come back!'

The boy swiftly located M. Durham – as much an expedience as an act of charity – and experienced the novelty of sharing the information with the girl, in the only way she appeared able to receive it. 'She's two miles away,' he said, with his own mouth. 'Heading north.'

Aggie Hanwell sat down on her bum in the wet sand. She rolled something in her hand. The boy looked at it and learned that it was a periwinkle – a snail of the sea! He recoiled, disliking those things which crawled and slithered upon the earth. But this one proved broken, with only a pearlescent nothing inside it.

'So it was all a lie,' Aggie said, throwing her head back

dramatically to consider the sky. 'Plus one of them's got my number. I've done nothing wrong but still Melly's gone and left me and one of them thing's been following me, since the pier – even before that.'

'If you've done nothing wrong,' Bill Peek said, solemnly parroting his father, 'you've nothing to worry about. It's a precise business.' He had been raised to despair of the type of people who spread misinformation about the Programme. Yet along with his new maturity had come fresh insight into the complexities of his father's world. For didn't those with bad intent on occasion happen to stand beside the good, the innocent, or the underaged? And in those circumstances could precision be entirely guaranteed?

'Anyway, they don't track children. Don't you understand anything?'

Hearing this, the girl laughed – a bitter and cynical cackle, at odds with her pale little face – and Bill Peek made the mistake of being, for a moment, rather impressed. But she was only imitating her elders, as he was imitating his.

'Go home,' he said.

Instead she set about burrowing her feet into the wet sand.

'Everyone's got a good angel and a bad angel,' she explained. 'And if it's a bad angel that picks you out' – she pointed to a craft swooping low – 'there's no escaping it. You're done for.'

He listened in wonderment. Of course he'd always known there were people who thought in this way – there was a module you did on them in sixth grade – but he had never met anyone who really harboured what his anthro-soc teacher, Mr Lin, called 'animist beliefs'.

The girl sighed, scooped up more handfuls of sand, and

added them to the two mounds she had made on top of her feet, patting them down, encasing herself up to the ankles. Meanwhile all around her Bill Peek's scene of fabulous chaos was frozen – a Minotaur sat in the lap of stony Abe Lincoln and a dozen carefully planted IEDs awaited detonation. He was impatient to return.

'Must advance,' he said, pointing down the long stretch of beach, but she held up her hands, she wanted pulling up. He pulled. Standing, she clung to him, hugging his knees. He felt her face damp against his leg.

'Oh, it's awful bad luck to miss a laying-out! Melly's the one knew where to go. She's got the whole town up here,' she said, tapping her temple, making the boy smile. 'Memoried. No one knows town like Melly. She'll say, "This used to be here, but they knocked it down," or, "There was a pub here with a mark on the wall where the water rose." She's memoried every corner. She's my friend.'

'Some friend!' the boy remarked. He succeeded in unpeeling the girl from his body, and strode on down the beach, firefighting a gang of Russian commandoes as they parachuted into view. Alongside him a scurrying shape ran; sometimes a dog, sometimes a droid, sometimes a huddle of rats. Her voice rose out of it.

'Can I see?'

Bill Peek disembowelled a fawn to his left. 'Do you have an Augmentor?'

'No.'

'Do you have a Complementary System?'

'No.'

He knew he was being cruel – but she was ruining his

concentration. He stopped running and split the visuals, the better to stare her down.

'Any system?'

'No.'

'Therefore no. No, you can't.'

Her nose was pink, a drop of moisture hung from it. She had an innocence that practically begged to be corrupted. Bill Peek could think of more than a few Pathways boys of his acquaintance who wouldn't hesitate. As the son of personnel, however, Bill Peek was held to a different standard.

'Jimmy Kane had one – he was a fella of Maud's, her main fella. He flew in and then he flew out – you never knew when he'd be flying in again. He was a captain in the army. He had an old one of them . . . but said it still worked. He said it made her nicer to look at when they were doing it. He was from nowhere, too.'

'Nowhere?'

'Like you.'

Not for the first time the boy was struck by the great human mysteries of this world. He was almost fifteen, almost a man, and the great human mysteries of this world were striking him with satisfying regularity, as was correct for his stage of development. (From the Pathways Global Institute prospectus: 'As our students reach tenth grade they begin to gain insight into the great human mysteries of this world, and a special sympathy for locals, the poor, ideologues, and all those who have chosen to limit their own human capital in ways that it can be difficult at times for us to comprehend.') From the age of six months, when he was first enrolled in the school, he had hit every mark that Pathways expected of its pupils – walking, talking, divesting, monetizing, programming, augmenting – and so it was all the more shocking to find himself face to face with an almost nine-year-old so absolutely blind, so lost, so developmentally debased.

'*This*' – he indicated Felixstowe, from the beach with its turd castings and broken piers, to the empty-shell buildings and useless flood walls, up to the hill where his father hoped to expect him – 'is nowhere. If you can't move, you're no one from nowhere. "Capital must flow."' (This last was the motto of his school, though she needn't know that.) 'Now, if you're asking me where I was born, the event of my birth occurred in Bangkok, but wherever I was born I would remain a member of the Incipio Security Group, which employs my father – and within which I have the highest clearance.' He was surprised by the extent of the pleasure this final, outright lie gave him. It was like telling a story, but in a completely new way – a story that could not be verified or checked, and which only total innocence would accept. Only someone with no access of any kind. Never before had he met someone like this, who could move only in tiny local spirals, a turd on a beach.

Moved, the boy bent down suddenly and touched the girl gently on her face. As he did so he had a hunch that he probably looked like the first prophet of some monotheistic religion, bestowing his blessing on a recent convert, and, upon rewatching the moment and finding this was so, he sent it out, both to Mr Lin and to his fellow Pathways boys, for peer review. It would surely count toward completion of Module 19, which emphasized empathy for the dispossessed.

'Where is it you want to go, my child?'

She lit up with gratitude, her little hand gripped his, the last of her tears rolling into her mouth and down her neck. 'St

Jude's!' she cried. She kept talking as he replayed the moment to himself and added a small note of explanatory context for Mr Lin, before he refocused on her stream of prattle: 'And I'll say goodbye to her. And I'll kiss her on her face and nose. Whatever they said about her she was my own sister and I loved her and she's going to a better place – I don't care if she's stone cold in that church, I'll hold her!'

'Not a church,' the boy corrected. 'Fourteen Ware Street, built 1950, originally domestic property, situated on a floodplain, condemned for safety. Site of "St Jude's" – local, outlier congregation. Has no official status.'

'St Jude's is where she'll be laid out,' she said and squeezed his hand. 'And I'll kiss her no matter how cold she is.'

The boy shook his head and sighed.

'We're going in the same direction. Just follow me. No speaking.' He put his finger to his lips, and she tucked her chin into her neck meekly, seeming to understand. Re-starting, he flagged her effectively, transforming little Aggie Hanwell into his sidekick, his familiar, a sleek reddish fox. He was impressed by the perfect visual reconstruction of the original animal, apparently once common in this part of the world. Renamed Mystus, she provided cover for his left flank and mutely admired Bill Peek as he took the traitor Vice-President hostage and dragged him down the Mall with a knife to his neck.

After a spell they came to the end of the beach. Here the sand shaded into pebbles and then a rocky cove, and barnacles held on furiously where so much else had been washed away. Above their heads, the craft were finishing their sallies and had clustered like bees, moving as one back to the landing bay at the encampment. Bill Peek and his familiar were also nearing the end of their journey, moments away from kicking in the door to the Oval Office, where – if all went well – they would meet the President and be thanked for their efforts. But at the threshold, unaccountably, Bill Peek's mind began to wander. Despite the many friends around the world watching (there was a certain amount of kudos granted to any boy who successfully met the President in good, if not record, time, on his first run-through), he found himself pausing to stroke Mystus and worry about whether his father would revoke his AG after this trip. It had been a bribe and a sop in the first place – it was unregistered. Bill had wanted to stay on at the Tokyo campus for the whole summer, and then move to Norway, before tsunami season, for a pleasant fall. His father had wanted him by his side, here, in the damp, unlit greylands. An AG 12 was the compromise. But these later models were security risks, easily hacked, and the children of personnel were not meant to carry hackable devices. That's how much my father loves me, Bill Peek thought hopefully, that's how much he wants me around.

Previously the boy had believed that the greatest testament to love was the guarantee – which he had had all his life – of total personal security. He could count on one hand the number of times he'd met a local; radicals were entirely unknown to him; he had never travelled by any mode of transport that held more than four people. But now, almost adult, he had a new thought, saw the matter from a fresh perspective, which he hoped would impress Mr Lin with its age-appropriate intersectionality. He rested against the Oval Office door and sent his thought to the whole Pathways family: 'Daring to risk personal security can be a sign of love, too.' Feeling inspired, he split the visual in order to pause and once more appreciate the human mysteries of this world slash how far he'd come.

He found that he was resting on a slimy rock, his fingers tangled in the unclean hair follicles of Agatha Hanwell. She saw him looking at her. She said, 'Are we there yet?' The full weight of her innocence emboldened him. They were five minutes from Ware Street. Wasn't that all the time he needed? No matter what lay beyond that door, it would be dispatched by Bill Peek, brutally, beautifully; he would step forward, into his destiny. He would meet the President! He would shake the President's hand.

'Follow me.'

She was quick on the rocks, perhaps even a little quicker than he, moving on all fours like an animal. They took a right, a left, and Bill Peek slit many throats. The blood ran down the walls of the Oval Office and stained the Presidential seal and at the open windows a crowd of cheering, anonymous well-wishers pressed in. At which point Mystus strayed from him and rubbed herself along their bodies, and was stroked and petted in turn.

'So many people come to see your Maud. Does the soul good.'

'How are you, Aggie, love? Bearing up?'

'They took her from the sky. Boom! "Public depravity." I mean, I ask you!'

'Come here, Aggs, give us a hug.'

'Who's that with her?'

'Look, that's the little sis. Saw it all. Poor little thing.'

'She's in the back room, child. You go straight through. You've more right than anybody.'

All Bill Peek knew is that many bodies were lying on the ground and a space was being made for him to approach. He stepped forward like a king. The President saluted him. The two men shook hands. But the light was failing, and then failed again; the celebrations were lost in infuriating darkness . . . The boy touched his temple, hot with rage: a low-ceilinged parlour came into view, with its filthy window, further shaded by a ragged net curtain, the whole musty hovel lit by candles. He couldn't even extend an arm – there were people everywhere, local, offensive to the nose, to all other senses. He tried to locate Agatha Hanwell, but her precise coordinates were of no use here; she was packed deep into this crowd – he could no more get to her than to the moon. A fat man put a hand on his shoulder and asked, 'You in the right place, boy?' A distressing female with few teeth said, 'Leave him be.' Bill Peek felt himself being pushed forward, deeper into the darkness. A song was being sung, by human voices, and though each individual sang softly, when placed side by side like this, like rows of wheat in the wind, they formed a weird unity, heavy and light at the same time. *'Because I do not hope to turn again . . . Because I do not hope . . .'* In one voice, like a great beast moaning. A single craft carrying the right hardware could take out the lot of them, but they seemed to have no fear of that. Swaying, singing.

Bill Peek touched his sweaty temple and tried to focus on a long message from his father – something about a successful inspection and Mexico in the morning – but he was being pushed by many hands, ever forward, until he reached the back wall where a long box, made of the kind of wood you saw washed up on the beach, sat on a simple table, with candles all around it. The singing grew ever louder. Still, as he passed through their number, it seemed that no man or woman among them sang above a whisper. Then, cutting across it all like a stick through the sand, a child's voice wailed, an acute, high-pitched sound, such as a small animal makes when, out of sheer boredom, you break its leg. Onward they pushed him; he saw it all perfectly clearly in the candlelight – the people in black, weeping, and Aggie on her knees by the table, and inside the driftwood box the lifeless body of a real girl, the first object of its kind that young Bill Peek had ever seen. Her hair was red and set in large, infantile curls, her skin very white, and her eyes wide open and green. A slight smile revealed the gaps in her teeth, and suggested secret knowledge, the kind of smile he had seen before on the successful sons of powerful men with full clearance – the boys who never lose. Yet none of it struck him quite as much as the sensation that there was someone or something else in that grim room, both unseen and present, and coming for him as much as for anybody.

Two Men Arrive in a Village

Sometimes on horseback, sometimes by foot, in a car or astride motorbikes, occasionally in a tank – having strayed far from the main phalanx – and every now and then from above, in helicopters. But if we look at the largest possible picture, the longest view, we must admit that it is by foot that they have mostly come, and so in this sense, at least, our example is representative; in fact, it has the perfection of parable. Two men arrive in a village by foot, and always a village, never a town. If two men arrive in a town they will obviously arrive with more men, and far more in the way of supplies – that's simple common sense. But when two men arrive in a village their only tools may be their own dark or light hands, depending, though most often they will have in these hands a blade of some kind, a spear, a long sword, a dagger, a flick-knife, a machete, or just a couple of rusty old razors. Sometimes a gun. It has depended, and continues to depend. What we can say with surety is that when these two men arrived in the village we spotted them at once, at the horizon point where the long road that leads to the next village meets the setting sun. And we understood what they meant by coming at this time. Sunset has, historically, been a good time for the two men, wherever they have arrived, for at sunset we are all still together: the women are only just back from the desert, or the farms, or the city offices, or the icy mountains, the children are playing in dust near the chickens or in the communal garden outside the towering apartment block, the boys are lying in the shade of cashew trees, seeking relief from the terrible heat – if they are not in a far colder country, tagging the underside of a railway bridge – and, most important, perhaps, the teenage girls are out in front of their huts or houses, wearing their jeans or their saris or their veils or their Lycra miniskirts, cleaning or preparing food or grinding meat or texting on their phones. Depending. And the able-bodied men are not yet back from wherever they have been.

Night, too, has its advantages, and no one can deny that the two men have arrived in the middle of the night on horseback, or barefoot, or clinging to each other on a Suzuki scooter, or riding atop a commandeered government jeep, therefore taking advantage of the element of surprise. But darkness also has its disadvantages, and because the two men always arrive in villages and never in towns, if they come by night they are almost always met with absolute darkness, no matter where in the world or their long history you may come across them. And in such darkness you cannot be exactly sure whose ankle it is you have hold of: a crone, a wife, or a girl in the first flush of youth.

It goes without saying that one of the men is tall, rather handsome – in a vulgar way – a little dim and vicious, while the other man is shorter, weasel-faced, and sly. This short, sly man leaned on the Coca-Cola hoarding that marked the entrance to the village and raised a hand in friendly greeting, while his companion took the small stick that he had, up to that point, been chewing, threw it on the ground, and smiled. They could just as well have been leaning on a lamp post and chewing gum, and the smell of borscht could have been in the air, but in our village we do not make borscht – we eat couscous and tilefish and that was the smell in the air, tilefish, which even to this day we can hardly bear to smell because it reminds us of the day the two men arrived in the village.

The tall one raised his hand in friendly greeting. At which moment the cousin of the wife of the chief – who happened to be crossing the long road that leads to the next village – felt she had no choice but to stop opposite the tall man, his machete glorious in the sun, and raise her hand, though her whole arm shook as she did so.

The two men like to arrive in this manner, with a more or less friendly greeting, and this might remind us of the fact that all humans, no matter what they do, like very much to be liked, even if it's for only an hour or so before they are feared or hated – or maybe it would be better to say that they like the fear that they inspire to be leavened with other things, such as desire or curiosity, even if, in the final analysis, fear is always the greater part of what they want. Food is cooked for them. We offer to make them food or else they demand it, depending. At other times, on the fourteenth floor of a derelict apartment building covered in snow – in which a village lives vertically – the two men will squeeze onto a family's sofa, in front of their television, and watch the new government's broadcast, the new government they have just established by coup, and the two men will laugh at their new leader, marching up and down the parade ground in that stupid hat, and as they laugh they will hold the oldest girl watching television by her shoulder, in a supposedly comradely manner but a little too tightly, while she weeps. ('Aren't we friends?' the tall, dim man will ask her. 'Aren't we all friends here?')

This is one way they arrive, though they did not arrive that way here, we have no televisions here and no snow and have never lived above the level of the ground. And yet the effect was the same: the dread stillness and the anticipation. Another girl, younger, brought the plates of food for the two men, or, as is the custom in our village, the single bowl. 'This is good shit!' the tall handsome stupid one said, scooping up tilefish with his dirty fingers, and the little sly one with the face of a rat said, 'Ah, my mother used to make it like this, God rest her shitty old soul!' And as they ate they bounced a girl each on their laps while the older women pressed themselves against the compound walls and wept.

After eating, and drinking – if it is a village in which alcohol is permitted – the two men will take a walk around, to see what is to be seen. This is the time of stealing. The two men will always steal things, though for some reason they do not like to use this word and, as they reach out for your watch or cigarettes or wallet or phone or daughter, the short one, in particular, will say solemn things like 'Thank you for your gift' or 'We appreciate the sacrifice you are making for the cause', though this will set the tall one laughing and thus ruin whatever dignified effect the short one was trying to achieve. At some point, as they move from home to home, taking whatever they please, a brave boy will leap out from behind his mother's skirts and try to overpower the short, sly man. In our village this boy was a fourteen-year-old we all used to call King Frog, owing to the fact that once, when he was four or five years old, somebody asked him who had the most power in our village and he pointed to a big ugly toad in the yard and said, 'Him, King Frog,' and when asked why explained, 'Because even my father is afraid of him!' At fourteen he was brave but reckless, which was why his wide-hipped mother had thought to tuck him behind her skirts as if he were a baby. But there is such a thing as physical courage, real, persistent, very hard to explain, existing in tiny pockets here, there, and everywhere, and though almost always useless it is still something you don't easily forget once you've seen it – like a very beautiful face or a giant mountain range, it sets a limit somehow on your own hopes for yourself – and, sensing this, maybe, the tall, dim one raised his gleaming machete and, with the same fluid yet effortless gesture with which you might take the head off a flower, separated the boy from his life.

Once blood has been shed, especially such a quantity of blood, a kind of wildness descends, a bloody chaos, into which all the formal gestures of welcome and food and threat seem instantly to dissolve. More drink is generally taken at this point, and what is strange is that the old men in the village – who, though men, have no defence – will often now grab at the bottles themselves, drinking deeply and weeping, for you need courage not only to commit bloody chaos but also to sit by and watch it happen. But the women! How proud we are, in retrospect, of our women, who stood in formation, arms linked the one to the next, in a ring around our girls, as the tall, dim man became agitated and spat on the floor – 'What's wrong with these bitches? Waiting is over. Any longer and I'll be too drunk!' – and the short, sly one stroked the face of the chief's wife's cousin (the chief's wife was in the next village, visiting family) and spoke in low, conspiratorial tones of the coming babies of the revolution. We understand that women stood so in ancient times, beside white stone and blue seas, and more recently in the villages of the elephant god and in many other places, old and new. Still, there was something especially moving about the pointless courage of our women at that moment, though it could not keep two men from arriving in the village and doing their worst – it never has and never will – and yet there came that brief moment when the tall, dim one seemed cowed and unsure, as if the woman now spitting at him were his own mother, which passed soon enough when the short, sly one kicked the spitting woman in her groin and the formation broke and bloody chaos found no more obstruction to its usual plans.

The next day the story of what happened is retold, in partial, broken versions that change depending very much on who is asking: a soldier, a husband, a woman with a clipboard, a morbidly curious visitor from the next village, or the chief's wife, returned from her sister-in-law's compound. Most will put a great emphasis on certain questions – 'Who were they?' 'Who were these men?' 'What were their names?' 'What language did they speak?' 'What marks were on their hands and faces?' – but in our village we are very fortunate to have no rigid bureaucrats but instead the chief's wife, who is, when all is said and done, more of a chief to us than the chief has ever been. She is tall and handsome and sly and courageous. She believes in the *ga haramata*, that wind which blows here hot, here cold, depending, and which everybody breathes in – you cannot help but breathe it in – though only some will breathe out in bloody chaos. For her such people become nothing more than *ga haramata*, they lose themselves, their names and faces, and can no longer claim merely to bring the whirlwind, they are that wind.

This is of course a metaphor. But she lives by it. She went straight to the girls and asked for their account and found one who, encouraged by the sympathetic manner of the chief's wife, told her story in full, the end of which was the most strange, for the short, sly one had thought himself in love and, afterward, laying his sweaty head on this girl's bare chest, had told her that he, too, was an orphan – though it was harder for him, for he had been an orphan for many years rather than mere hours – and that he had a name and a life and was not just a monster but a boy who had suffered as all men suffer, and had seen horror and wanted now only to have babies with this girl from our village, many boy babies, strong and beautiful, and girls, too, yes, why not girls! And live far from all villages and towns, with this army of children encircling and protecting the couple all their days. 'He wanted me to know his name!' the girl exclaimed, still stunned by the idea. 'He had no shame! He said he did not want to think that he had passed through my village, through my body, without anybody caring what he was called. It is probably not his real name but he said his name was –'

But our chief's wife stood up suddenly, left the room, and walked out into the yard.

Kelso Deconstructed

The people are Kelso and Olivia, a couple. The setting a shabby rented room on the Bevington Road, in Portobello. It was Kelso's room, until five weeks ago, when Olivia moved in. Kelso is from Antigua, originally. He is a carpenter. Olivia is a trainee nurse from Jamaica. They are engaged to be married, although they will never marry: by the time the next sentence arrives it will be Saturday 16 May 1959, the last day of Kelso's life. One thing about the last day of our lives is we almost never know that it is the last day – from here stems 'dramatic irony' – and no more did Kelso know it. His mind was full of the pain in his thumb and the heat in the room. The break was unusual, low down, in the final joint: underneath the doctor's makeshift splint he could feel the bone still moving. The pain was hard to bear, somehow shameful. He didn't want to bore her complaining about a thumb, nor to be unable to open a window while she looked on, but the frame had been painted carelessly, it was sealed shut, there seemed to be no moving it. She stood at his shoulder, desperate for air on a sweltering afternoon. Kelso put the hub of his palms to the sash. Braced himself.

'P'raps you should just call this Mr Reynolds and ask him . . .'

'Oh, I will, Livvy, I certainly will.'

They both knew he'd do no such thing. Reynolds considered himself a saint for renting to them in the first place ('Plenty wouldn't!') and never lifted a finger on any account, not even for the Irish on the second floor. Now as Kelso bent his knees a little, to get more purchase on the frame – and Livvy begged him not to bother with it – his right hand slipped, bumping the thumb against the lock. His moan was long and pitiful. Bent over himself, he watched her step forward and force the sash. Little flecks of dry paint went flying to the carpet. The air moved a little, not much.

'Hoo! Strong woman I'm marrying!'

'If you want to see true true muscle, go see about my Auntie P in Dalton. She pick you up! High up! If you think *I'm* strong you don't know.'

'See, maybe I propose to the wrong Miss Ellington after all that. But wait one minute: what does this Auntie P look like I wonder?'

Olivia cracked up: 'Broad as three men side by side.'

'I see, I see . . .'

Kelso put his good hand round Olivia's waist and leaned into her. They looked out together, over Notting Hill. It was Whitsun Bank Holiday, hottest day of the year so far, and the streets were relatively empty, excepting the little half-moons of people gathered outside the doors of the pubs and the dominoes place on the next corner. He was conscious of the fact that many people were presently boarding trains and coaches on their way to the seaside or other pleasant locations. He could not offer her any of that, but still their Saturdays were precious, as they are to all working people, and when the hammer fell on his thumb in the workshop on Wednesday that had been his first thought:

let this be brief. Whatever this is about to be, pain, doctors, pharmacy visits, all of that business – Lord pray let it be done with by Friday night. But all this morning, wandering with Olivia through the Saturday market, as he smiled and nodded whenever she pointed out a nice basket, or a good-looking mango, or a brass carriage clock, his only true thought had been: thumb thumb thumb thumb. It was the same when his younger brother, Mal, came by. His little brother had not neglected to bring the ginger wine, he arrived laden with fresh gossip from back home, and amusing, off-colour stories from the factory floor at McVitie's, but Kelso could not get any of the usual pleasure from it. He sat glumly in his chair, his hand very still, pressed between his thigh and the armrest, a copy of the *Reader's Digest* open in his lap. It was left to Mal to commandeer Kelso's precious Dansette, upon which he now played half a dozen melancholy jazz standards – 'I'll be Seeing You', 'They Can't Take That Away from Me', 'The Very Thought of You'– each one about loss and death and love, and therefore thematically consistent with what was about to occur.

But Kelso, caught in the slipstream of life, without the hindsight of either reader or author, could think only of his own pain, which, by this point, was not stabbing, sharp or occasional but radiating, unceasing, and mind-consuming. He let Mal dance with Olivia. He did not sing along or make much comment on anything. He did his best to read the words in his lap. It was a foreign story, Russian, translated and made shorter for the convenience of the working man, and it concerned the death of a lawyer. For this reason, Kelso had turned to it with a special interest: the law was his own aspiration; he hoped one day to afford to study it. But the story was heavy going. It had come to him by way of a costly subscription – two bob for the year – the price of which he tried not to think of too often, for if he did he knew he would cancel it. The trouble was, it was near impossible to say at what point a working man, such as himself – for whom every shilling counted – had even *done* two bobs' worth of reading, and it was also very difficult to say whether the things you *did* read – even if you read them cover to cover, every month, and for the full year – were worth two bob in the first place. Words were obviously not like records or silk handkerchiefs or the sorts of spiffy waistcoats he happened to favour – the only other material items on which he had ever considered spending two bob. No, words were not like that. What were they like? There just didn't seem to be any way at all of knowing. He didn't imagine even the rich and educated knew the answer, any more than he did – they just didn't miss the two bob either way.

This particular story he had been reading for a month at least, and freely admitted to himself that he was not really following it, but still he liked it well enough for those sentences that seemed, every now and then, to be about himself – that is about Kelso – although of course he understood that they actually referred to this mysterious Russian character, Ivan. Who lived in a house Kelso could not visualize, in a time and a place surely too distant in history to feel real to any reader, be he working man or no. Last week, the story had felt especially far from his own reality – almost to the point of being incomprehensible. What he had thought would be a tale of the law had turned out to be more about pain, excruciating pain and miserable death, and each paragraph felt like a swamp you were being forced to wade through. Yet now that he was in such unexpected pain himself he found certain lines shot out at him directly, as if addressed to him only, with personal intent:

The people around him did not understand or would not understand it, but thought everything in the world was going on as usual.

Yes, he felt just like that!

It was almost four. A look passed between Olivia and Kelso which Mal, good-humoured by nature, did not take personally, corking what was left of the ginger wine and tucking the bottle jauntily under his arm. And his brother, who loved him dearly, and saw him do this, did not take any offence. You shared what you could and took back what you needed, for nobody was living like the Queen of England over here, were they?

'Well, I'll be seeing you, Kel, man,' said Mal. He would not, not ever again, but wasn't to know. Kelso, for his part, was not eager to move his hand from its rigid position and left the good-byes to Olivia, who gave her almost brother-in-law a kiss on each cheek, closed the door behind him and then took her place in the armchair next to Kelso. They had two such chairs. She considered this one of the many advantages of marrying a carpenter. What foolish people threw out, Kelso could mend and make good, and Olivia's contribution was a pair of decently sewn slip covers, and if only the room itself were bigger they'd have had many more people round to admire their handiwork. She looked over at her love, still reading, clearly in pain. She picked up her sewing basket, a little dutifully. On Saturdays, by mutual agreement, they tried to 'uplift' themselves and not waste the precious hours on too much foolishness. Kelso did his book reading and she tried to busy her hands in a way that was not labour, that had something leisurely about it. But leisure did not come naturally to her, and if he caught her darning a sock or hemming a curtain he certainly didn't like it, and let her know he didn't. Why couldn't she understand that she deserved a 'weekend' as much as any other Londoner? He was especially adamant about her doing nothing useful during bank holidays, so now she passed over the torn skirt that sat on the top of her basket – and urgently needed her attention – reaching instead for a perfectly pointless piece of embroidery she'd been working on almost as long as Kelso had been reading his *Digest*. It was a pretty oval, text in the middle and bluebells round the edges, and, if she ever finished, it would sit on the wall above their chairs, a touch of home:

> *Words are to be taken seriously.*
> *I try to take seriously acts of language.*
> *Words set things in motion.*
> *I've seen them doing it.*

But she had only got as far as the second 'seriously', which she now noticed contained a foolish error – it was missing a 'u' – and so began, with a little sigh, to unpick it.

A few minutes later, Kelso surprised her, raising his knee, letting his book fall shut, standing up suddenly.

'Livvy, the thing is we must get out of here. It's hot as the Devil in here! And, you know, it's not too late.'

By which he meant that they were not too late for Speakers'
Corner, where they usually went after Mal had left them: it
was part of their weekend of uplifting and betterment. Some
people thought of Saturday only as sweet relief, as domino
and rum, but Kelso didn't think that way, and she was glad he
didn't, even if there were times she wished he didn't frown so
on going to the pictures. 'All you will see at the Odeon is
advertisements for America and I can tell you I've been to
America and it is not at all what is advertised!' Olivia found
this sentiment unusual, and very impressive. At the same
time, she never enquired too deeply into his American experience, suspecting, from little things he had said here and there,
that it had been a moment in his life when the Devil was pulling on his collar. But that had been another woman's problem,
and a different Kelso. 'And every Saturday around five,' she
had written home to her mother, in the letter that contained
the news of her engagement, 'we go to Speakers' Corner
down in Hyde Park, to hear all the people talking.' It was both
uplifting and less painful than the Odeon on her pocketbook.
Still, her girlfriends thought it an odd habit. They had no
experience of a man with a plan, who thought beyond tomorrow, but Kelso was ten years older than Olivia and her friends
and the difference told: he had learned to save his money. One
day he would be a lawyer in a strange white wig. Now she
picked up her bag and put on her hat and checked her change
purse for the train fare. They stepped out into the hot streets
in their shiny shoes, their clean, formal clothes, and she felt a
certain pride. Going to the Corner of a Saturday was like everything else, it was like the way she and Kelso dressed, the
way they walked, the careful precision of their habits – all

these things marked them out, in her mind, as a special couple, with a special destiny.

The man in front of them was old and white, quite bald, with only a little grey hair on each side and dark furry eyebrows. Evidently a French poet. He stood on a simple slatted box, the kind used to transport those fruits that fall ill at the least lack of air, and he peered into the crowd with interest, as if trying to discern what type of audience this might be at his feet. This suggested to Olivia that there was more curiosity than authority about him. She liked people like that. Kelso himself was like that.

'The thing about narrative,' said the speaker, on the crate, 'is that it is inherently inauthentic. It is prearranged information in a certain pattern. It will always have a motive. It will always be a manipulation . . .'

'Look at his bushy brows!' crowed a foolish woman behind Olivia. 'Don't he look just like a snowy eagle!'

'Oh, hush up and listen,' said Olivia, but under her breath, and without turning round. 'If you listen you might even learn a little something.' (Kelso restricted himself to sighing and looking up, with renewed scholarly intensity, at the curious figure on the crate.)

'And if this manipulation,' the Frenchman continued, 'if it comes from the right, well, then we call it propaganda, and if from the left we tend to consider it not only humane but beautiful. We think of literature as humane and beautiful. It matters very much who the "we" is in this proposition. I am a French poet. I do not include myself in that "we". And would it not be better to place the humane and even the *human* to one side for the moment and to deal only with material facts? To say, with me, like an incantation: the darkness, the street light, the stiletto knife, the puncture, the wound, the blood, the cobbles, the tarmac, the kerb . . .'

The speaker went on like this for some time. It was a hot day to be near so many other bodies, listening to such a forceful oration. Kelso and Olivia were familiar with oration – as we have seen, they came to hear it most Saturdays – but they were not accustomed to the heat, at least not here, in England, where they had learned to wear sweater vests and cardigans with everything, no matter what the early-morning sun on their windowpanes implied. Now each stripped off a layer, which Kelso hung over his left arm, crooked to a ninety-degree angle, and found the elevation helped the pain. Olivia, tiring a little of the French poet, turned her attention to an American voice on her left, which turned out to belong to a woman not unlike her own grand-mother: the same lion's face, the same wealth of hair.

'The function,' said this woman, 'the very *serious* function of racism is distraction. It keeps you from doing your work. It keeps you explaining, over and over again, your reason for being.' *Your reason for being!* thought Olivia, and gripped Kelso's good hand a little tighter. The fresh pressure was a counter-balance to the pain in his other hand, he could use the one to distract from the other. This worked for a moment. Then the pain re-established itself, more persistent than ever. He could not attend to this woman. He could barely attend to anything.

At a quarter past six, a great flock of swallows took flight from the top of Marble Arch and swept over the crowd, so low that many crouched – including most of the speakers – after which everybody straightened up again, the speakers carried right on speaking, the tricky thing became knowing when to leave. Neither Kelso nor Olivia ever wanted to be the one to say: 'Let's go.' They had to place the decision outside of themselves, in the weather or some other external cause, for to leave was to give up on betterment, or to suggest betterment was less fun than the pictures, or the market, or a million other, easier things.

'How's your thumb? It pain you still?' asked Olivia, in a sudden leap of inspiration. He was holding his left hand to his chest with his right like someone about to say something terribly sincere, an oath, maybe, or a profession of love.

'Oh, Livvy – it's murder!'

They walked back to the station. At the entrance, a newspaper boy was changing the hoarding poster from today's headline: 'SIGNS AND SYMBOLS!' to tomorrow's: 'FORESHADOWING!' Kelso stopped, rolled a thin cigarette and lingered a while so as to read the front page, which this particular lenient newspaper boy – they were not all like that – did not stop him from doing. As the boy busied himself cutting the strings off several towers of the *Daily Express*, Kelso read of venality, poverty, crime, corruption, murder.

'Madness, madness, everywhere,' he murmured, feeling almost as sorry for the world as he did for his mangled thumb.

'Kel, the train soon come!'

An old woman sat opposite them. She had a pink scarf tied over her grey curls, too much powder on her nose, and a look on her face like she wished them both dead. Olivia thought: Oh Lord, even if I hated *anyone* that much I wouldn't want to look that way as I did it! How ghoulish this woman looked, snarling like that – almost like Enoch himself. Olivia turned to Kelso to see if he'd noticed but his head was bowed, he held his wrist as if to cut the blood from the offending hand, so that he might feel nothing at all. Olivia raised her own gaze fixedly to the illustration of the Piccadilly Line, choosing to focus on the names of the stops – Cade Bambara, Ponge, Tolstoy, Morrison – mouthing them silently to herself, finding this calmed her, and at the next station the ghoulish woman got off.

By the time they got home it was past eight. They'd walked through a summer rowdiness – music from every pub, women dressed as they shouldn't be, drunk lads revving up their mopeds – and Olivia was more than ready for her bed. The heat in the room was stifling. She hung her coat and hat on the little hook Kelso had fashioned for the purpose, turned back and found him pacing the small space, his coat still over his arm, his hat crushed in his good hand. She watched him dump his small change out on the table, where it could serve as evidence against a botched robbery. He took another turn around the room, moaning.

'You want me to go with you?'

'No, Livvy, no point in two people in a waiting room when only one is sick.'

She put his hat back on his head. Warned him she might be asleep by the time he got back.

*

It was already mostly drunks in St Mary's and ragged, homeless white people, the existence of whom still very much surprised him, even after five years in the country. He sat slightly apart from them all, his thumb pressed between his knees. An hour went by. A nurse called him into a small corner, marked off with curtains on a rail. She undid the bandage and the splint and showed him the correct way to hold the throbbing joint until a Dr Rooney arrived. Another hour passed. Then a surprise – a woman! Livvy claimed there were two women doctors at her hospital, but he had never seen an example for himself. This one was alarmingly young: her pale ears poked through her poker-straight hair, she looked like a schoolgirl. He asked her if that was an Irish name. She nodded, but said nothing more. She took his thumb, pressed it between her own thumbs to align it, then set it in a fresh splint, with a fresh bandage, all the time speaking very little to him, but going about her business with a serious intent and also a delicacy Kelso admired: she did not look at him, for example, when he yelped. As she worked, he watched her. He wondered whether he himself could have been a doctor, had he been dealt different cards. What she was doing did not seem so very distant from carpentry.

'There you are,' she said, and smiled, for the first time. She passed Kelso her prescription. It was formatted strangely, like an email from one writer to another:

From: YoungIrishWriter@gmail.com
To: OlderEnglishWriter@yahoo.com

Not having any academic background in 'creative writing' I've never really understood the injunction 'show don't tell', but now I think maybe it's communicating the same basic concept – that there are some ideas impossible to understand or accept as direct statements, but just marginally, fleetingly comprehensible in the form of stories. At times, I do wonder if there's something slightly dishonest in this approach, that it turns the novel into a kind of parable or illustration of a precept instead of an honest narrative.

Kelso took it gratefully. He thanked the good doctor and started for home. He walked down the Harrow Road and over the Grand Union Canal. Water went with water in his mind. The green and murky lagoon behind his great-aunt's house – where he and his cousins had often picnicked in the black sand and swum in the early evenings – seemed to lie, in his mental geography, at the other end of a channel of water connecting Antigua to this grey canal beneath his feet, and stretching all the way back to the New World, to the Potomac and the Hudson, both of those so very cold and filthy. Perhaps if he had lasted longer in the States – or in that bad American marriage – he might think of white sands and warm waves, but all his American water had been on the East Coast. Stacking shipping containers at Vesey Street might put a man off water for life he supposed, yet without water you cannot be reborn, and daring to cross an ocean one more time had been his own form of rebirth, a second baptism. He had tried America, then he had tried England – how many could say that? And he was still standing, despite many setbacks and missteps. He felt he knew his own worth. Livvy knew it. Mal knew it. The lads at work knew it . . . No, no, he wasn't at all like the Russian gentleman in the story, unloved and disrespected, and it was a shame to have such an idea walking home alone, it was really very silly and morbid. He turned his mind to Olivia. He considered the whole back line of her body and how he would soon press into it and sleep, feeling less pain than he'd experienced these past four days. Oh, if there was anything wonderful about pain it was the moment when you stopped feeling it! When feeling nothing became its own incredible gift. And in a few more days, God willing, he'd be back there in that place, with everybody else, in the land of nothing, of no pain. Yet if he could only wipe those American years, that woman . . . the wrong path, the years wasted. But that was the kind of pain you just had to live with. He'd give everything on this earth to be twenty-one again, to step into the river of time with Olivia, but have them both be the same age, and have everything else exactly as it was now, except with those lost years rolled tight in his fist, not yet unravelled.

He was walking back from St Mary's. He was minutes from his door. It was just after midnight. They were 'white youths'. They liked to make trouble for 'spades'. They'd been drinking. They were not affiliated with Mosley's crowd in any official capacity. They'd just left a fight at a party. Some of them became career criminals, and went to jail years later, for crimes presumably considered more serious by the state: robbery, fraud. Many stayed in the area, died in the neighbourhood, unmolested by the law. The one who did it, who held the stiletto knife and did the stabbing, he was twenty at the time, a merchant sailor. He has a name, it was known to the police within half an hour of the event. But he, too, died unmolested by the law, living a long, quiet life in the suburbs, in Hillingdon. Ended up as a painter-decorator. After his death, his stepdaughter told a newspaper of how he used to smash up her Bob Marley records. If you align his witness statement to the left-hand margin, it looks like a poem:

Fifty yards up the road
we had sorted out our little argument
and turned to go back to the party.

When we reached the corner we saw this
black man
lying on the pavement clutching his chest.
Two spades — that's what we call coloured men here —
were standing beside him.

We decided to get out of it fast.
It was not our business.
Then when we saw how serious it was
we decided to come clean and tell the lot.

I had a lot of bloodstains on my clothes.
For that matter, all my clothes
have blood on them.

You know, from one fight or another.
Old stuff.
We fight a lot here.
Life is like that in Notting Hill.

The police took away my clothes but I was in the clear.

In the poem, all our British names are used – Black, Spade, Coloured – but no man appears to claim them. These are not names for Kelso. They name rather a certain kind of malignancy in the brain of Patrick Digby, the poet–murderer, whose name, like all proper names, describes him perfectly. Patrick Digby was the man capable of thinking that way and of writing this poem. But a lot of people could write it. It's amazing how many. The possibility of its composition reoccurs, at different moments in history, in different places. The details change but the deep structure remains. A form of tragic verse in which the slaughtered man is a kind of object and only the poet keeps his proper name.

Kelso's blood spilled upon the poet Patrick Digby, he got it on his knife and his suit, and it stained, too, that pair of gentlemen from the diaspora – referred to in the poem – who, upon spotting Kelso bleeding out in the street, knelt by his still-breathing body and tried to come to his aid. A passing taxi driver took the three men to St Mary's, where, an hour later, Kelso died. He had no last thoughts. Last thoughts are for bourgeois Russian deathbeds, in comfortable town houses, where false friends and colleagues take tea in the next room and ponder what vacancies and opportunities your death might afford them. When you are stabbed in the street that kind of poetry is in short supply. There is what you see and what there is. You are weighed down by facticity. The last words written by the poet Francis Ponge concerned the very table he was writing them on: *O Table, ma console et ma consolatrice, table qui me console, ou je me consolide.*

The blood, the cobbles, the tarmac, the kerb.

*

You can watch Pathé newsreel of Kelso's funeral. Over a thousand people came – they lined the streets. At some juncture, on its long journey to our digital era, the footage of this event lost its sound and became a silent funeral, without language, without commentary, open to interpretation. To be noted is the great mix of people, black and white, young and old, men and women, as if Kelso's death concerned all these people, as if they were all somehow in relation to it. As if, contra the poet–murderer Patrick Digby, Kelso Cochrane was precisely everybody's business. Alone, a little anxious, not knowing anyone intimately, I shake hands and make small talk with the ministers who stand at the doors of the church, and spend a long time slowly reading and rereading the *Thought for the Day*, which is pinned to the parish noticeboard:

> *Action against racial*
> *Hierarchies can proceed*
> *More effectively when it has been purged*
> *Of any lingering respect for*
> *The idea of race.*
> Reverend Paul Gilroy

A young Marxist in dark glasses is wandering around the funeral with a newspaper. He wants to insist on relation. As he moves through the crowd he is proselytizing, he is saying:

> *Brothers and Sisters and Comrades,*
> *Don't you see that if you refuse*
> *To enter into each other's stories –*
> *If you refuse to admit a relation between you –*

Why, then you hand capitalism its finest victory?
Sweet music it is to the foreman,
To hear that the Blacks and the Poor Whites,
And the Irish and Navvies and Skivvies,
Have no relation to each other!
That they can make no common cause!
Sweet music!

The mourners glance shiftily at the Marxist as he moves between them, a cigarette pressed tight between his lips, his Socialist rag held front page outwards upon his chest. Is it time to hit back? Time to unite? Who decides? What would either course of action look like? In silence, the mourners read the headline, and then return to their silent conversations, sometimes frowning a little or turning away with embarrassed smiles, not sure what to make of it, as ideology, but certain that a funeral is not quite the right place for whatever this is. They have come to mourn a man, a human being, member of the local community, Olivia's fiancé, Mal's beloved big brother, this young son of Antigua, cut down – as the vicar tells the congregation – in the prime of his life. The coffin, shouldered by five white men, files past the two black ministers, and into the hearse. The huge crowd follows on foot, headed to Kensal Rise Cemetery: a black, brown and white column of people, some stony-faced, others chatting and smiling, as if walking behind a float to carnival. The time for transforming a dead man into words, into argument and symbol and history, this moment will surely come, but the mourners think it in bad taste that this young Marxist should ever have come here this morning, to the funeral of Kelso Cochrane. They have turned from him, they leave him behind, but though I walk with them, still I am curious about the young Marxist, and stop to take a copy of his paper when he hands it to me, and stand for a moment in the street, admiring the brazen headline: ALL THE WORLD IS TEXT.

Blocked

What nobody gets is that the conditions were unusual, basically unrepeatable. I was young, full of beans. I'd just *created* beans, cars, grassland, Post-it Notes, the white rhinos, everything else, created them in an immanent sense, having replaced nothing with something, which – as even my harshest critics will admit – then led to everything else, beans included. Point is, it was a 'first thought, best thought' kind of a situation. And when you create something out of nothing at such a tender age it's just a lot to take on, psychologically. It's a lot. That's not really why I withdrew, though. I was always going to withdraw, deep into myself. I understand that others do it differently, but for me, at the time, it was a principle. I found it self-evident that the thing should have its own engine, its own life, its own propulsion. It wasn't a theoretical pose – it was something I felt at a gut level. I still feel that way, really. Because otherwise where's the risk? You can't be in every household, sitting at a person's shoulder, asking: *So, what do you think of what I did there, or here – does that work for you? Can I do anything to improve your experience?* I mean, you can, but you're on a hiding to nothing. No matter what anybody tells you, the underlying principle is not consumer satisfaction. There's no feedback loop. You make it, you put it out there, you deal with the consequences. A lot of times they're going to hate it and hate you for creating it, but if you can't deal with hatred you've got no business being in the game in the first place.

Having said that, there are a lot of things in there that I simply wouldn't do now, or not in the same way, if I had the opportunity to do it all again, from scratch. I'd be the first to admit that. When you're young you try to prove you can do it all, anything – you throw everything and the kitchen sink in there! You're profligate! You've got this sense of unlimited potential. You think you contain multitudes, and in my experience you kind of *do*, at that age, because you're still sufficiently flexible to contain multitudes, you haven't drawn lines around your shit yet and there is still something ineffable about you, something that can make space for whatever is *not* you. But that crowd inside thins out. Lord, does it thin out. For example, yesterday I was mooching around in my long johns when I had a thought, I wondered: What does it feel like to be a bat? Now, that sort of thing used to be a fruitful line of imaginative enquiry for me. But I didn't know yesterday and I still don't know. I've made my peace with it: I don't expect to know how a bat feels about anything any time soon. But I know how *I* feel. That's what you get left with, in the end: a very precise and intricate sense of how you yourself feel. Which is not nothing. When I started out I had no earthly idea about *that*. Now I know. People talk about checking back in and maybe reworking some things and adapting others and so on and so forth but those people do not know my mind, they do not know what I can face and what I find too much to deal with at the current time. Only I can know that. It might sound a little nuts, coming from me, but a lot of people could do with being a lot less judgemental.

Sometimes I am asked: How do you keep from getting depressed? Given the state of things. Given that it looks like the something you got started is on the brink of collapsing back into nothing? The answer has changed over time. I used to think parallel projects were the solution. Just keep on creating parallel projects and moving between them and then you never have time to get really down on any one of them. 'Okay, sure, that's a roiling mess – but this one has got something, oh, it's really got something!' Of course, as soon as I felt one of these parallel projects was going well, a moment later I'd hate it, and want to move on to the next thing, which would then provide its own complications, and so on. And all the time some part of me understood that dropping one ball was a problem unlikely to be resolved by simply launching a whole load of other balls into the air. But for a while it worked, psychologically, for me. I can't speak for others. To me, it was beautiful to move between these parallel projects, never getting bogged down, not feeling defined by one way of doing things, feeling light, feeling free . . . Doesn't mean it wasn't avoidant behaviour. I'm not a fool, I know when I'm being avoidant. But some of the most sublime things emerge as vehicles of distraction. Really depends on how you look at it. These days, I love a fragment. I don't think of a fragment as flawed or partial in any way. It's the completist model that got me into such trouble in the first place. Now I praise the half-done, the unfinished, the broken, the shard! Who am I to turn my back on the fragment! Who am I to say the fragment is insufficient!

At the same time, I *am* depressed. The difference is these days I just say it out loud:

I AM DEPRESSED.

At a certain point, given the way things are, it's a fair and rational response. The fact that I even have to defend the emotion tells you all you need to know about how large the distance has become between my mind and all other minds. It's really an issue. Mostly, when people talk to me about what they think and feel about it all, and their own relation to me or all of it, I willingly participate – as in, I will and do listen – but I remain keenly aware that in practical terms nine times out of ten we are not discussing or thinking about the same entity in any way, shape, or form. On the one hand, I feel totally alienated by their interpretations; on the other, they find my perspective impossible even to *identify* never mind actually engage with. We're talking straight past each other. Have been for the longest time. Which is legitimately depressing, a word by the way that is not mine and which I hate to use, and only sound out now so as to be able to know you all better, and to share in your reality. Contrary to reports, naming things was not and never will be my bag. I myself never put things in bags. I barely recognize the existence of 'bags', at least not as a collective noun. Nor would I ever, for example, have thought up the separate denomination 'animal' – and then treated it as if it were a licence! – no more than I would *ever have presumed* to describe a category called 'emotions' or consider them as something you 'have' – like a stone or a stereo – and then go on to define them morally, depending on what they did to my face muscles or tear ducts. That shit is not on me. Yet I still have to deal with people speaking to me as if all of that is reality – I have to at least appear to take it seriously. And I'm sure that behaving in this false way, in such bad faith, day in and day out, is what has inhibited me somewhat, and contributed to this sense of blockage. It doesn't make me want to take new risks, that's for damn sure, or start afresh with something big. To what end? Everything gets twisted. Control is an illusion. I certainly have never personally drawn a line around 'France', but at a certain point, when you've got this critical mass of belief in 'France' – on the part of those who believe they are 'citizens of France' and indeed separate entities each from the other – well, what are you going to do about it? Tell them to take another look? *Pardon, monsieur, madame – le monde n'est pas ce que vous pensez!* Please. 'People' see what they want to see.

Instead of self-medicating, I recently got involved with a dog. Judge that however you may wish but I'll tell you right now I've never been happier. I no longer feel any anxiety as I pass by what I don't want to go back to, because each day I have a purpose, a direction, I really know what I'm doing. I've got to take dear old Butler for a walk and let him sniff all the things he likes to sniff without hurrying him or chivvying him along in any way at all. That takes up half the day. And when me and Butler are done there's even a little time to flit through the parallel projects, never finishing any one of them, never raising any to the level of perfection, but feeling okay about all of them, neither delighted nor desperate. It's a life. I'll take it. There aren't many who do what I do but whenever I happen to come across a significant colleague – not any of the hacks, but one of the few I admire and more importantly whom I like – whenever I happen to run into one of these esteemed colleagues, maybe at the deli on Mercer, and we stop and greet each other, and they see me with Butler, I know very well what they're thinking. Me who used to be so high and mighty, shuffling round the neighbourhood with this dumb-looking coonhound. What the hell happened? Well, they can think what they like. I'm just very, very happy waiting patiently for this old dog to sniff the many things it likes to sniff, while my colleague smiles at me in that certain way, like there's something satirical about me now. I actually have a sense of humour, and I understand how funny it must look: me, with a dog! It's really a bad joke on myself, given that I once thought – when dogs initially appeared on the scene – that *this* time I had really managed to (inadvertently) offer, to the 'people', a revelatory illumination, a deep and renewing insight into the true nature of reality, when of course the exact opposite lesson is what they all seem to have taken from it. 'That's my dog,' you hear them announcing, pulling their leashes tight, with that smug look of ownership on their stupid faces. 'Yeah, sure, you can pet my dog.' There's no control, none whatsoever. I don't worry: I've let it all go. I'm happy, I get to spend my days with a fantastic dog, I am no longer concerned whether or not I am the only soul left in existence who knows what a dog means and what it is for.

The Canker

At the time of the Usurper, Esorik and her people lived beyond the mountains and had done for some time. Their island fell like a teardrop from the north-east side of the land, into that broad sea that was at once their livelihood, their conceptual foundation, and their best argument for independence – physical and spiritual – from the mainland, of which, in truth, they were an integral part. On her Labour days, Esorik was a fish-salter. She greeted the Ekalbia on the docks, and showed them where to hang their huge silk nets. Stronger women than she emptied the nets; cannier women negotiated with those bloody-minded, green-eyed nomads over the price. Esorik's task was to heave the little grey fish by the spadeful onto her pallet of squat rectangular tubs, then pack them in salt. Sometimes, as she did this, the sun set in pink and purple bands across the horizon, and on those occasions, she felt almost grateful for Labour days and understood their purpose. The rest of the time she smelled of fish. Salt got into any little cut on her hands. She looked forward to her final cycle.

On Praxis days, she was a teacher: she taught the children of her district how to tell stories and more importantly the names of the various forms. The Snake with the Tail in its Mouth. The Resurgence. The Straight Arrow. The Sinking Ship. As Praxis, it was rather pathetic, being so close to Esorik's own Anima – which was storytelling itself – but she was good at it and besides she had little choice: her Anima was almost all of her. She possessed no hidden talents. She could not add, build, invent anything real, configure, organize or lead. She knew brilliant women on the island, many, friends of hers, whose lives were the soul of variety, who, on their Labour days, built bridges, and when their Praxis came, designed civic systems or sat on justice committees. She knew women who did all of this and then, to display their Anima, danced through the streets with coloured ribbons streaming from their joints, singing founding songs at least as old as the paving beneath their feet. But Esorik was a storyteller pure and simple. Who had learned – though not without some struggle – as much as anyone can know about the packing of fish in salt.

When the Usurper was first put in power, Esorik behaved like most island people. She called him the 'Usurper' although he had been chosen, however misguidedly, by the people, and she encouraged everyone in her circle to spit on the floor three times whenever his name was mentioned. She presided over a circle of five, two males, two females and herself, and they were now in their fourth cycle, Esorik having had her children fifteen years earlier, whom Lohim and Seg had then cared for – while she educated herself and worked in the world outside their compound, and spread her passions thinly within it. But Lohim and Seg, men in their thirties at the time of the Usurper, found the moment for their own divergence had come, and of course now dear Leela and Ori were pregnant in their turn. At the very moment the Usurper took power, then, Esorik was deep into the satisfied, ripened period of her life:

re-greeting her children, saying farewell to Lohim and Seg, seeking new lovers and fresh passion, and preparing to put her island duties aside – Labour, Praxis and Anima entire – so as to care for the soon-to-be-born. And it was because of this fullness in her own existence, perhaps, that she had experienced the Usurper, initially, as only the intrusion of the worldly on the intimate. She did not see why the story of her life or anybody's should be so profoundly distorted by this monstrosity from the mainland. In her time she had met many people of the outer archipelagos who, when you traded with them, did nothing but bemoan the corruption of those who ruled over them, and often seemed, to Esorik – who did not believe she lived in a comparable state of emergency – distracted by their own misery, monomaniacal in their fixation upon a justice beyond their grasp. Yes, Esorik had known many such people, and felt profoundly sorry for them, but in her innocence, she had never imagined she could so easily become one of them. For a period, she had an urge to petulantly refuse the new situation. At the same time, some part of her always understood this reaction to be both childish and typical of an older woman who had seen many cycles. She kept it to herself.

Like most people on the island, she considered it her civic duty to supervise, within her circle, the construction of a bier – in their case a bier of walnut and silver, the building of which took fourteen days – and then to lay their youngest member upon it, bound and blindfold, topped and tailed by candles. With at least a million others, they rolled out their bier on the assigned night, down to the closest shore. As had been hoped, the circumference of the island was thus lit up, and it was visible from the mainland – an entire generation mute and alight – of which vision, the mainland took note, as did the Usurper, and none of it made a whit of earthly difference. Yet she felt better. It made sense to the storytelling part of her, which, as we have seen, was almost all of her, even though these old forms of story, popular on the island, appeared to the mainland to be antique and idealistic and the very reason the Usurper had found such favour in the first place. The Usurper, for his part, placed his youngest girl – his circle was only young girls – on a gimcrack bier, covered in flowers, in the sun-struck middle of the day, and gave a vulgar public address as he loomed over her body, in which he ridiculed men like Lohim and Seg and the very concept of the cycle. Like many others, Esorik recognized this address as the oldest story form of them all – The Father Who Eats His Young – but knowing a thing, and accepting it calmly – as only another rhythm in the infinite cycle – are very different matters.

She became enraged. Like many storytellers, she entered his mind, even though, on the island, this remained wholly prohibited: a gift long ago set aside so that other gifts might flourish. His mind was exactly as everyone had expected, it writhed and it oozed. It was an abomination. But it was satisfying to have that fact confirmed at least, and soon details were everywhere, circulating as songs and riddles, filthy jokes and rhyming curses, for though Esorik told no one of what she saw, many others, motivated by the common rage, were far less circumspect, and having so little respect for what they uncovered inside the Usurper, felt within their rights to spread the news far and wide, without caution, heedless of the island's oldest taboo. The dock women, for example, with whom Esorik packed fish – whose labour was, by necessity, eight tenths of their cycle – sang the ugly new songs as they worked, cackling and whooping at the end of each vicious line, as familiar now with the workings of the Usurper's mind as any seer or storyteller. Such barbarism became general. Hunting the white hart returned to fashion. Friends of Esorik, people she'd known for years, turned their circles into hunting parties and chased that elusive animal through its habitat, stabbed it in multiples of seven – seven strokes each – and then stood over the poor beast's heaving belly as it bled out into the earth and over their shoes. Behaviour like this had not been seen for thirty cycles or more, but as long as the Usurper venerated the white hart and believed it to be the source of his power, the creatures themselves were considered fair game, killed in reality to repudiate a symbol.

Esorik did not sing the songs or hunt the harts, but years later, looking back on that tragic period, she reflected on the many ways, small yet significant, in which she had contributed to the breaking of all the cycles she had ever known. She remembered that when teaching The Canker in the Rose, for example, teaching it over and over – it became the only form she could bear to impart – the children would get bored of the repetitive lesson, and stray from their circle under the tree, gathering instead in smaller groups to sing the ugliest songs and imagine the ritual dismemberment of the Usurper, or the fiery destruction of the mainland and the emergence of a self-determining island, fantasies they had heard adults in their own circles repeat, and which they now retold, with great verve and excitement, as if they were mere fairy tales from the fireside . . .

Yet when Esorik had heard the children speak in this way, she had not stopped them, in fact she'd often encouraged them, even laughed, for the Usurper was one of whom you could say anything, think anything. He was a universal licence. Cycles became meaningless. Everybody circled only around him. And when he singled out the Ekalbia, for living nowhere and trading with everyone, some part of Esorik, at the time, in that atmosphere of madness, had found it a satisfying story that so many of the Ekalbia's little curraghs should have sunk a mile from the mainland, drowning Ekalbia men, women and children, their compact sable bodies appearing for months later at the shoreline, their bright green eyes as still as sea-glass. All because the Usurper had not granted them the right to dock on one of the stormiest nights of the year, which tragic tale had only proved her point, it simply demonstrated the ruthlessness and barbarism of the Usurper, and of all who followed him – and what else is a story for?

For the King

Arriving in Paris from Strasbourg, I rushed from Gare de l'Est to meet my friend, V, who had agreed to take me for a late dinner. It would be his plan and his treat, all I had to do was meet him on Rue Montalembert at 9.15, outside my hotel. I'd been working, and reaching my hotel with five minutes to spare, took the opportunity to rush upstairs to change, with that strange urgency sometimes brought to dressing for friends, especially if, like V, they are themselves beautiful and well-dressed. I took off the high-waisted jeans and severe shirt buttoned to the neck, replacing them with a long silk dress, black, but dotted with yellow flowers, a crisp denim jacket, big white trainers, and some very red lipstick. I ran back downstairs. I had informed my friend, in an email, that I was exhausted with talking, that I had talked myself to death, and he should do all the talking, on all subjects, no matter how small. I wanted to hear everything, even the dullest minutiae of his life. The moment we saw each other, however, we fell into a mutual unburdening, speaking over each other in a series of overlapping waves as we walked through the city: his work and mine, his family and my own, the situation in Europe versus the situation in America, gossip about mutual acquaintances, and any other interesting developments that had occurred since we'd last seen each other, a year earlier, in London. I'd been surprised to discover that he was in Paris at all, and now he explained he'd won a bursary, which had installed him as an artist-in-residence at the university, so that he was presently surrounded on all sides by academics. He found them curious people: never able to say a word without qualifying it from fifteen different angles. To listen to them, he said, is to be confronted with a mass of verbal footnotes. And, by contrast, whenever I open *my* mouth to speak, unthinkingly, as you know I always do, saying whatever comes into my head, everybody looks utterly horrified. Or else, they tell me I'm brave. But it's awful to be told you're brave when you had no idea that you were taking a risk!

The day had been unseasonably hot – twenty-eight degrees in October – and by the time we got to the restaurant it was still warm enough to eat outside. We were led to our seats by a waiter of incredible beauty who immediately became a topic of conversation. He was black, very young, slender yet muscular, and moved like a dancer between the tables, openly flirting with many of the male diners, including my friend. And how is your boyfriend? I asked V, pointedly. Your boyfriend of twenty years' standing who lives by the sea? How is he? Oh, he is well, replied my friend, with a look of mock-formality upon his face. He continues to be very well. Although we are in an interesting new phase of our relationship where I begin to notice that it's better if I tell him only about the amusing encounters – where the sex went wrong or something ludicrous happened – whereas if I have an actual connection with someone, it's better if I keep that to myself, because if I tell him, he goes quiet, he feels hurt in some way. Though of course for me it is exactly the *real* connections that are most worth talking about and therefore those are the ones that I feel most guilty about keeping from him, because by omitting them I omit a part of my real, lived experience. It's a conundrum!

Listening to V made me smile. When he asked me why I said I was thinking about all the middle-aged people in the world, presently torturing themselves as they observed – mainly via lifestyle articles in their Sunday papers – the polyamory of the young, which led them to wonder whether, after twenty years of marriage, it was not too late to introduce the idea of opening up their own relationships in some way. V laughed. In my culture, he said (making the word 'culture' sound satirical) that conversation is radically sped up. Two men get together and are absolutely blissful. The happiness goes on and on. But then they check the calendar and lo and behold three months have gone by and it's time to consider an open relationship . . . The beautiful waiter returned to ask what we wanted to drink, and a moment later, in the most charming way possible, expressed the usual French disbelief in the existence of a vodka Martini. V picked a bottle of white wine instead and sat back in his chair as the waiter left, admiring him as he returned to the kitchen. I told V that I used to think people were wildly jealous of what they perceived as the sexual freedom of men like him, but now I felt that most people did not really want sexual freedom after all, not at least if it meant having to grant the same freedom to those whom they wanted for themselves. No, what we wanted at least as much as sex was the opportunity to recreate, replay and improve upon our old family dramas, in a new house, with new mothers and fathers, except this time around your parent would be someone you could also have sex with, as Freud pointed out. One of Freud's greatest insights in fact was that there was nothing more perverse than bourgeois married life. V nodded vigorously as he tore at a piece of bread. Amen to that! These days, I continued, when I look at the figure of the ageing lothario, for example, jumping from girl to girl, what I really see is a man desperately looking to be mothered. I wonder what happens to that instinct in men like you? V sighed. It's possible, he said, that the very definition of the gay man is he who has had enough mothering to last a lifetime.

Over our main course, we discussed Parisian sex clubs and orgies. A good friend of V's attended them with some regularity and had given him a full report, which he now passed on to me. I was very interested in the little lockers where you put your clothes and also the fact that so many people kept their socks on. What interested me most, however, was the idea of treating other people like objects, but before I could get very far down this line of enquiry, my friend interrupted me. I didn't say objects, he said, I was talking of body parts, of orifices and members, which is very different. Those organs all have the same capacity for pleasure, and are equally ignorant of who 'owns' them. It's you who moralize, bringing up the difference between objects and persons. And anyway, what matters at an orgy is not a different attitude to people but a different relationship to time. *You* – V pointed a finger at my chest – are altogether too conscious of time. It distorts your view of many things. Even your own family drama – I mean of course the age gap between your parents – has always been understood by you as a fundamental inequality between them. But I am in a relationship with a similar gap and rarely think about it. You choose to think it so important because time is your preoccupation. For example, I can remember once telling you about a busy day of sexual encounters I'd had around the city and you said you couldn't really understand daytime sex on the grounds that it 'wasted time'. Time that could be more profitably spent working! V threw his hands up in despair. It was my turn to laugh and also to protest – in the spirit of these things I had been at least half joking. Yes, persisted V, but at the core of it there was a truth. I think of sex, any act of sex, as something that ignores and in fact obliterates time, so that sexual pleasure never is and never could be a waste of time, because it negates time entirely!

After we had cleaned our plates – in my case to the point you would never know it had ever had food on it – the waiter returned and ignored our mutually feigned ambivalence towards dessert. We ordered a platter of mixed cheeses and a giant crème brûlée. I tried to defend myself by pointing out that a woman's life so often feels dictated by time: biological time, historical time, personal time. I thought of my friend Sarah who once wrote that a mother is a sort of timepiece for a child, because the time of a child's life is measured against the time of the mother. A mother is the backdrop against which a child's life is played out. It might be understandable if such a time-weighted being found it hard to allow pleasure to entirely obliterate time. V pretended to seriously consider this counter-argument but then as soon as I'd stopped speaking presented a substantial list of women artists, past and present, who'd delighted in daytime sex, although how he knew this about them he didn't explain. Maybe you're simply too English, suggested V, and I conceded the point.

By the time V paid the bill it was past midnight, but as we'd started late we felt we hadn't quite had enough of each other, so proceeded to Café de Flore, ordered more wine, and considered all the exercise we would have to do the next morning to counter the effects of the wine, cheese and sugar on our middle-aged physiques. I asked him how he felt about ageing. V frowned and asked why was I worrying about the subject, I looked exactly the same. But that's what friends always say, I replied, and they're not lying, but it's a delusion of familiarity. I don't feel that you've aged or that any of my friends have aged but that can't possibly be the case. Yes, said V, but you really haven't or not that much, so it's offensive and boring – not to mention in bad taste – to hear you complain about something that barely affects you. I reached out to pinch V's waistband, and pointed out the – what? Twenty-nine inches it had always been? Twenty-eight, he cried. It's twenty-eight! Please get it right and also make a note so you remember! I promised to do so. With his iPhone, V took a selfie of the two of us, which we eagerly bent over the screen to study, only to discover that neither of us looked anywhere near as young as we'd imagined. But if we were white, said V, a little glumly, putting his phone back in his pocket, it would already be a lost cause so at least we have that to be thankful for. Still, one day I know that I will look in the mirror and see one of those very, very old men you see selling fish by the river in rural Chinese villages, and you will look and find whatever the Jamaican equivalent of that is. It will happen very abruptly. We'll have been thirty-seven for twenty years and then all of a sudden we'll both be a hundred and five.

By this point we were quite drunk. Our conversation staggered around haphazardly, like an old fool stumbling down the road, paying no attention to the cracks in the pavement. We wondered what young people overhearing us might make of our ancient conceptual divisions – straight, gay, bi, men, women – how ridiculous we must sound to them. I put it to V that in revolutions young people are generally always right and old people almost always wrong, but V rolled his eyes and said: Well, if that were true we'd all still be living in spiritual cults in the San Fernando Valley. I was wrong at twenty, he murmured, and I'm still wrong now. Being wrong is a lifelong occupation. We fell quiet and watched the street traffic. Since my last visit to Paris a new kind of electric scooter had invaded the city, like the child's version but twice the size and made of metal. People left them abandoned wherever and whenever they felt like, then took them up again, using an app on their phones, translating this new technology into ancient Parisian habits, so that as we sat in Café de Flore we could watch several pairs of picturesque lovers go by, two bodies on a single scooter, helmetless, holding each other, as they had previously done on Vespas and on bikes, in 2CVs and horse-drawn carriages, or on the back of a farmer's trailer, snug upon bales of hay.

It was very late. We launched into a cruel assessment of previously pretty young men we'd once known, and then back again to age in general, to May and December romances, and whether either of us still found people in their early twenties attractive. V felt that absolutely yes, he did, although it was sometimes very hard to listen to their conversations, while I had to admit that my apparently typically feminine preoccupation with time made the young more or less invisible to me now, they were young enough to be my children and I could see them in no other light. Something about this fact depressed me: with age, and despite myself, even my desires had become civilized and appropriate. To cheer me, V described an older French artist of his acquaintance. She was eighty years old, travelled all over the world to museums showing her work, and always took with her a little case on wheels, filled with lingerie. She prided herself on regular one-night stands with men in the art world, many of whom were in their twenties. I told V that was the Frenchest thing I ever heard. He agreed and we raised a glass to this octogenarian adventuress. As we counted out our euros, we discussed another old artist, a man this time, who had recently lost his gallery because of a series of exploitative sexual relationships with younger men. What interested me in V's account of the matter was that 'everyone' had known that the man in question was a sentimental and submissive bottom, who had a habit of becoming sloppily emotionally attached to his young lovers, or victims – depending on your point of view – sending them flowers, crying down the phone, et cetera. That the 'perpetrator' happened in this case always to be the penetrated, never the penetrator, was an aspect of the case that played no part whatsoever in the newspaper accounts, for whom this detail was of no interest, either because it made no difference whatsoever to his guilt or innocence, or perhaps because it was structurally invisible. But so much of life is structurally invisible, I noted, and has no way of fitting into the external accounts of our lives. Our lives are so different on the inside. We can never express their full particularity and strangeness in public, their inner chaos and complexity. There are always so many things it proves impossible to say! Yes, said V, but at the same time you can't concede everything to the public account, to what people see or think they understand. In a completely different arena, for example, here in Paris I am Chinese. The public part of me, that is my face, speaks for me before I can, and so in the public accounting, Chinese is what I am. I cannot walk the streets with a sandwich board explaining my birth, my nationhood, my culture, my history, the history of my country and so on. That would be exhausting, impractical. But neither do I concede to their external definition. You have to be careful how much of yourself you render to Caesar. Of course, I know what I am and given the time and space I can and will express the facts fully. Although in truth I don't bother very often. It may be a question of sensibility. I am always very amused, for example, by the sort of person who gets infuriated if you mispronounce their name! Everywhere I go in France people ask me if it's a long A in my name or a short one. They ask very anxiously, as if they know many people for whom this kind of thing matters enormously and they don't want to make the same mistake with me. I suppose, continued V, living peacefully in a society means understanding that the things others care about might mean nothing to you and vice versa. Do you know what I mean?

In lieu of an answer I told him a story about a party I once attended, at which a man called me by another woman's name all night, mistaking me for her, maybe because she did the same sort of work as me. I didn't correct him, though we had met many times before. I tried to find it in myself to be insulted, to feel as others feel, to care as they would care, but instead I felt a strange lightness, like I'd given myself the slip for the evening. V listened in silence and then took his linen jacket, which he had not needed all night, off the back of his chair. I think that's why I keep changing cities, he said, to keep on giving myself the slip.

On the walk back to my hotel, I wanted to tell one more story, about something that had happened on my train journey, earlier that evening, en route to Paris, but there was no easy way to introduce it, as it did not in any obvious way connect with anything else we had discussed, seeming to come from another reality. Yet I couldn't shake the sense that it was significant. As we retraced our steps through the city, gossiping and joking, in the back of my mind I kept seeking some way unobtrusively to turn to my story, without seeming like an egomaniac who did nothing but tell stories about herself, but before I could find a solution we arrived at the door of my hotel. We said our goodbyes, hugging each other tightly, and I ran up three flights of stairs, drunk and happy, grateful to have such a friend to whom one can say anything, without fear. But as I had this thought I remembered: I had not told him everything. I had not told him about the man with Tourette's on the train from Strasbourg. He had been around my age, though his hair was sparse and grey, and he wore a light brown mac over trousers and shoes of the same shade, as if an attempt had been made to shroud him in camouflage. *Pour le Roi!* the man said, every twenty seconds or so. *For the King!* Sometimes he repeated it at much briefer intervals, hardly pausing between repetitions of the phrase. He could not help but say it: the only choice before him was modulation. He could be very loud or not so loud. The woman next to him, in her sixties, whom I presumed to be his mother, alternated between enjoining him to speak less loudly and answering each repetition gently, without any sign of irritation: *Oui, oui . . . Oui, mon amour . . . Pour le Roi.* For a moment, my eyes met with hers: she and her charge were sitting right behind me. I had no doubt, looking at her, that she had been listening to those three words for many years, maybe decades. Perhaps mixed with other words at some earlier point, but perhaps not. The look she gave me I find hard to describe. It expressed no pain, shame or anxiety. It made no application for forbearance, pity or acceptance. It was neither defiant nor angry. It was not even especially tired. The face was completely neutral. This is it, her face said. This is my life.

The carriage was full. Realizing that the man would not stop, *could* not stop, each passenger – within a few moments of settling in their seats – reached for their earbuds, and thus entered a private world. I did the same. What might have been a torturous trip twenty years ago was now no trouble to anyone. There was a palpable sense of collective gratitude to technology: this evening it would allow us to be our best selves. We would not look over our shoulders, sigh, or privately pray for this benighted family to get off the train. We would smile and take our seats with a sympathetic look, signifying that we had no objection to sharing our space with the mentally afflicted. Where others surely listened to music or podcasts or movies or audiobooks, I chose 'brown noise', a warm static, turned up high, which allowed me to read a novel in peace, entirely uninterrupted. The time passed quickly. Before I knew it, I had arrived in Paris, eager to meet my friend, and taking off my earphones, was surprised to re-enter a reality I'd forgotten about, one that had persisted while I visited another. In this reality, time could not be sidestepped, avoided or obliterated. It could only be endured. For the man still had no choice but to say *Pour le Roi!* To repeat it every few moments, sometimes screaming it, sometimes not, while the woman at his side – who could so easily have stayed silent – offered each and every time her quiet, earnest response: *Yes, yes . . . Yes, my love . . . For the King.* Treating the statement not as something involuntary, essentially empty – like the yawp of an animal – but as a human utterance, which still carried some form of meaning, however small.

Now More Than Ever

There is an urge to be good. To be seen to be good. To be seen. Also to be. Badness, invisibility, things as they are in reality as opposed to things as they seem, death itself – these are out of fashion. This is basically what I told Mary. I said, Mary, all these things I just mentioned are not really done any more, and also, while we're on the subject, that name of yours is not going to fly, nobody's called Mary these days, it's painful for me even to say your name – actually, could you get the hell out of here?

Mary left. Scout came by – a great improvement. Scout is so involved and active. She is on all platforms, and rarely becomes aware of anything much later than, say, the three-hundredth person. By way of comparison, the earliest I've ever been aware of *anything* was that time I was the ten-million-two-hundred-and-sixth person to see that thing. There's evidently a considerable gulf between Scout and me. But that's why I am always so appreciative of her coming by and giving me news. Now, according to Scout, the news was (is?) that the past is now also the present. I invited her to pull up a stool at my mid-century-modern breakfast bar and unpack that a little for me. The light that afternoon was beautiful – from my place on the eleventh floor I could see all the way to the Hudson – and it filled me with optimism and an eagerness to be schooled. But Scout was cautious. Believing me incapable of either trans-historical thought or platform mastery, she placed a New York Sports Club tote bag on the counter and pulled out two puppets – home-made, insultingly basic. The first was a recognizably female human, although she had long arms, terribly long, at least three times the length of her body, and no nose. The other was a kind of triangular spindle with a smudgy face painted on both sides, trailing thread from its corners, which I could have sworn I'd seen someplace before. Scout's demonstration was quite detailed – I don't want to get into it all here – but the essence of it was: consistency. You've got to reach far, far back, she explained, into the past (hence the arms), and you've got to make sure that when you reach back thusly you still understand everything back there in *the exact manner* in which you understand things presently. For if it should turn out that you don't – that is, if, after some digging, someone finds evidence that present-you is fatally out of step with past-you – well, then, you'll simply have to find some way to remake the connection, and you've got to make it seamless. Not double-faced or double-sided (like this triangle-spindle guy) but seamless, because otherwise you are (and were) in all kinds of trouble. Seamless. *Seamless*. At which point we both got hungry and paused to order a couple of poké bowls.

'Here's a question for you re: consistency,' I said, putting my elbows on the counter. 'I know this woman who's a big fancy CEO, her name is Natalia Lefkowitz. She's totally squared the past with the present, is admired by all, and is not only seen to be good but actually does good in the world for many people, providing clean water and equitable job creation and maternity leave and plenty of other inarguable benefits for women here, there, and everywhere. But yesterday she got this message.'

I showed Scout the message, which I had received on my phone from someone called Ben Trainor, apparently an ex-boyfriend of Natalia, whose son – I mean, Natalia's son – was in my Kafka-and-Kierkegaard class a few years ago. According to this Ben Trainor, Natalia had liked to do things, in the very recent past, that were not consistent with her existence in the present. Stuff like sodomizing Ben Trainor while pretending to be his mother. Also calling him Daddy while he pretended to be holding her as a sex slave in a crawl space underneath her own East Hampton kitchen. At the time, they had both agreed to these oppositional kinks, but when they broke up it occurred to Ben that, although there was no contradiction between his own life and his intimate life (Ben worked as the general manager of a leather bar down on Rivington), there was surely a big old gap between how Natalia morally lorded it around in her professional existence and the weird shit she was into behind closed doors. In Ben's opinion, these dark desires 'went way beyond kink into problematic', which was the reason he was texting everybody in Natalia's address book to let them know.

'Scout,' I asked. 'Do you think she should be afraid?'

'Do I think she should be *afraid*? That's your question?'

'That's my question.'

Scout packed up her puppets and left, accusing me of flippancy and misjudging the current climate. We never even got to the poké. Sometimes I think I don't ask the right questions.

*

In my apartment building, as in many throughout the city, we have this new routine. We stand at our windows, all of us, from the second floor to the seventeenth, and hold aloft large signs with black arrows on them. The arrows point to other apartments. In our case, to the apartments of our colleagues at the university. The only abstainers are the few remaining Marxists (mainly in the history department, though we have a few in English and sociology, too) who like to argue that the whole process is fundamentally Stalinist. Which is like calling a child Mary. Who even uses that kind of language these days? Bendelstein, Eastman, and Waite are pointing at me. (A purely defensive move; I have done nothing wrong and am no one, and they are only trying to distract attention from themselves.) I am pointing at Eastman, in his dank little studio with the paisley carpet. Yes, since my illuminating discussion with Scout I have decided to join the majority of my colleagues in the philosophy department and point at Eastman, because who doesn't know about Eastman? How Eastman still has a job we really don't know. Not only does he not believe the past is the present, but he has gone further and argued that the present, in the future, will be just as crazy-looking to us, in the present, as the past is, presently, to us, right now! For Eastman, surely, it's only a matter of time.

I made a date with young Scout to go to the Forum. I felt we'd taken a wrong turn and I wanted to get our friendship back on track. I don't like this friction between the generations. We went to see *A Place in the Sun,* starring Montgomery Clift and Elizabeth Taylor. And Shelley Winters. I don't do that just to be cute: I genuinely feel bad for Shelley Winters. And if you've ever seen that movie, with its carnival of physical beauty – into

which poor, plain Shelley Winters has been placed as
counterbalance – you'll know that eight-point type is a fair and
accurate representation of the situation. The antihero of this
picture, by strange coincidence, is called Eastman. George
Eastman. He's played by Clift, who always makes me want to
type the word 'febrile'. It's as if he's so beautiful it's making him
ill. (When I mentioned this to Scout, she asked me why I
thought physically objectifying men was any different from
objectifying women. I had no answer. I returned to my pop-
corn.) George Eastman is the poor East Coast relation of a rich
California family that runs a big, successful bikini business.
Young Eastman grew up in his super-religious mother's Chris-
tian mission, proselytizing on the streets, probably shaking a
can for coins, but now he's come out West to ask his old Uncle
Eastman for a job. To cut a long story short, he falls in love with
two girls.

One is sweet, ordinary, sincere, lower-class: Shelley Winters. Shelley works with him on the factory floor, stuffing
bikinis into boxes, and happens not to be able to swim. (This
will become important later.) The other is hot-as-hell Elizabeth
Taylor: rich, upper-class, an Eastman family friend. Seeing as
he has no chance with Taylor, George gets things going with
Shelley, although relationships are banned in the factory, and if
they're discovered they'll both lose their jobs. Unfortunately,
Shelley falls pregnant. All of this is sometimes hard to follow
because the movie was made in 1951, and everything's buried
under the Hays Code. No one says 'pregnant' or 'I want an
abortion'. But, despite the polite cutaways and the euphemistic
language, you get the picture. Two unmarried people, with no
money, who hardly know each other, are about to have a baby

that neither of them wants. What to do? Shelley thinks the only solution is to get married. George doesn't want to. In the middle of this crisis, George bumps into Taylor again. This time she notices that he looks like Montgomery Clift and falls madly in love with him. So now Shelley is a problem. Gotta get rid of Shelley. But how?

To distract himself from the urgency of this question, George accepts an invitation to Taylor's parents' beach house and spends a weekend looking tanned and expensive, beautiful and happy, and not at all like a poor boy from Chicago who once walked the streets pleading with the lost and the sinful to join him in the bosom of Christ. Throughout this section of the movie, Scout kept leaning over to ask me, 'Did Montgomery Clift make this before or after his car accident IRL?' I really couldn't say. Whenever I thought it was after, I found myself noticing strange marks on his face: a cut on his cheek, or the scar from a huge laceration on his neck. But then when I thought it was before, his face looked perfect to me, as if God had taken Brando and Dean and found a way to combine them in a delicious man sandwich.

At a certain point, while George is trying to forget his troubles at the beach, Shelley Winters calls from the bus station and says that if he doesn't marry her right away she's going to come over to that beach house, publicly expose him, and fuck up his whole life. He makes his excuses to Taylor and her family and goes to meet Shelley. They head to the registry office, to get married, but it's closed. To calm her, George suggests a picnic, out in the woods, by the lake, and maybe that's when he remembers the time she told him she couldn't swim. He hires a rowboat – under a false name – and takes her out on the water, apparently with the full intention of killing her. And she does die that very day – in murky circumstances. The two of them argue in the little rowboat; it tips; they fall in. And the next thing we see is George dragging himself up the bank. Did he try to save her? Did he swim away? Did he force her head down, down, down into the water? Was it murder in the first degree? Or in some other degree? Was it even murder? We can't know. We'll never know. George heads back to his weekend paradise. Taylor's parents' black maid happens to be making lunch. You see her only three or four times, and she barely speaks, but let's just say that she had my full attention. I admired the way she acted as if she were fully invested in this drama unfolding at Taylor's parents' beach house even though, in my mental version, this fictional maid's fictional brother was one of the several thousand people who were lynched IRL in the first half of the twentieth century. Each time she appeared, I gave her a little improvised dialogue, whispering it into Scout's ear: 'Yes, miss, I'll bring the dessert out now. I mean, my brother was lynched not long ago, down in Arkansas, but I can see you've got bigger fish to fry – I'll get right on it.'

I let out a sort of ugly laugh as I said it, but I knew that nothing I could do in the present could ameliorate or change this fictional fact; no, all I could do was remember it, and tell myself I was remembering it – so that it wasn't forgotten, although with the mental proviso that suffering has no purpose in reality. To the suffering person suffering is solely suffering. It is only for others, as a symbol, that suffering takes on any meaning or purpose. No one ever got lynched and thought, Well, at least this will lead inexorably to the civil rights movement. They just shook, suffered, screamed, and died. Pain is the least symbolic thing there is.

There's a key scene, after my stoic maid has tidied lunch away, when Taylor and George and a load of other happy, young, rich people jump into a flashy speedboat that is leaving from the dock. Off they fly, whooping and smiling with their perfect American teeth. Meanwhile we, the anxious folk at Film Forum, stay on the dock, in the foreground, where a lone radio sits, and we listen to this radio as the happy young people frolic in the distance. We hear that Shelley Winters has died in a lake, that the police think it's murder, and they're closing in on the perpetrator. Which means that everyone on that boat, including Elizabeth Taylor, will soon know that George Eastman, aka Montgomery Clift, is guilty as sin, or is guilty to some, perhaps ultimately unknowable, degree. I found myself clutching Scout's hand, quietly weeping.

Later, on the way out of the cinema, Scout asked me if I instinctively sympathized with the rich and the happy. I said I didn't understand the question. She said, I'll put it another way: You instinctively sympathize with perpetrators instead of victims. Since that was less a question than a statement, all I could do was add a statement to her statement. I said, In our philosophy department at the university, we feel that, just as there are degrees of sin or error, there are degrees of sympathy. It's not a zero-sum game, or it used not to be, in the past. Well, there's your problem, Scout said. You're two-faced, you're looking the wrong way, and if you don't watch out you're going to find yourself beyond the pale.

She went off to catch the 1 train while I trudged back to my tower alone, making note of the fact that I'd be seeing no more films at the Forum for a spell, because it was closing for the summer so that a fourth screen could be built. That's what I need, I thought as I walked. A fourth screen. If I had a fourth screen, no reality could get through the cracks at all, I would be able to live only in symbol, and then surely everything would be easier. I was at LaGuardia Place before I noticed that almost everyone on the sixth floor was angling their arrows upward, directly at my apartment, though I wasn't even there. Montgomery Clift isn't rich or happy. He's guilty. I instinctively sympathize with the guilty. That's my guilty secret.

In the current climate, a high-school student wrote to me:

Dear Professor,

I am a high-school English student in South Bend, Indiana. I am quite intrigued by your use of metaphor in your recent piece in Philosophy Today. *But why did you choose to make the metaphor so obvious? And why would you not really take a stand (for or against) by specifically saying his name? And why would you choose to omit his name if you are taking a stand?*

Thanks,

A High-School Student

I wrote back:

Dear High-School Student,

Have you seen that video? It's a little like that. Some things are so obvious that subtle metaphor is impossible. In that video, for example, there was no point in being subtle about the state-funded violence inflicted on black people in this country: the only way was to show it explicitly. And when we saw all those people dancing in

*the foreground that was again the most obvious metaphor possible —
i.e., while you're watching these black people dance and entertain
you, other black people are dying.*

*As to your other question, I guess it seems to me that some
things are so low or evil or contemptible that they barely deserve a
name. Giving them a name would be to honour them more than
they deserve. See also 'he-who-shall-not-be-named'.*

Yours,

Professor

This did not particularly satisfy the high-school student, and
I can see why. Apart from anything else, I was the ten-million-
two-hundred-and-sixth person to watch that video, so my
opinions on it were easily discounted. And even the Lord himself called the Devil a variety of euphemistic names. Besides,
teenagers can sniff out the truth. (The truth is, I didn't want to
be deported.) The next week, making no reference whatsoever
to our previous exchange, the high-school student struck again:

*Hey, Professor, it's me, back to bother ya. My English teacher is
having us write a prompt comparing certain eras of literature and
what their authors would say in response to Hamlet's Quintessence
of Dust monologue. 99.9% of the authors are dead but you are
very much alive. I have pasted the monologue below just in case
you are not familiar with it. Thank you so much for your time!*

*I have of late, (but wherefore I know not) lost all my mirth,
forgone all custom of exercises; and indeed, it goes so heavily with
my disposition; that this goodly frame the earth, seems to me a*

sterile promontory; this most excellent canopy the air, look you,
this brave o'erhanging firmament, this majestical roof, fretted with
golden fire: why, it appeareth no other thing to me, than a foul
and pestilent congregation of vapours. What a piece of work is
man, How noble in reason, how infinite in faculty, In form and
moving how express and admirable, In action how like an Angel,
In apprehension how like a god, The beauty of the world, The
paragon of animals. And yet to me, what is this quintessence of
dust?

Thanks!

A High Schooler

I replied:

Dear High Schooler,

I'd say he's having a quarter-life crisis.

Best,

Professor

PS I know it's not much, but, on the other hand, as you say,
almost everybody else is dead and I am very much alive.

I bumped into someone on Bleecker who was beyond the pale.
I felt like talking to him so I did. As we talked I kept thinking,
But you're beyond the pale, yet instead of that stopping us from talking we started to talk more and more frantically, babbling
like a couple of maniacs about a whole load of things: shame,
ruin, public humiliation, the destruction of reputation – that

immortal part of oneself – the contempt of one's wife, one's children, one's colleagues, personal pathology, exposure, suicidal ideation, and all that jazz. I thought, Maybe if I am one day totally and finally placed beyond the pale, I, too, might feel curiously free. Of expectation. Of the opinions of others. Of a lot of things. 'It's like prison,' he said, not uncheerfully. 'You don't see anybody and you get a lot of writing done.'

If you're wondering where he would be placed on a badness scale of one to ten, as I understand it he is, by general admission, hovering between a two and a three. He did not have 'victims' so much as 'annoyed parties'. What if he *had* had victims? Would I have talked to him then? But surely in that case, in an ideal world – after a trial in court – he would have been sent to a prison, or, if you have more enlightened ideas about both crime and punishment, to a therapeutic facility that helps people not to make victims of their fellow humans. Would I have visited him in prison? Probably not. I can't drive, and besides I have never volunteered for one of those programmes in which sentimental people, under the influence of the Gospels, consider all humans to be essentially victims of one another and of themselves and so go to visit even the worst offenders, bringing them copies of the Gospels and also sweaters they've knitted. But that wasn't the case here. He was beyond the pale, I wasn't. We said our goodbyes and I returned to my tower, keeping away from the window for the afternoon, not being in the mood for either signs or arrows. I didn't know where I was on the scale back then (last week). I was soon to find out. Boy, was I soon to find out. But right now, in the present I'm telling you about, I saw through a glass, darkly. Like you, probably. Like a lot of people.

Then I made a mistake. This was yesterday. If you're any-thing like Scout, you probably heard about it already. (Scout emailed me fifteen minutes after it happened to commiserate and also to alert me to the fact that she would not be emailing me any more.) How it happened was: one of our poets said something beyond the pale. He is one of the newer poets – the musical kind – and so his words tend to go everywhere, floating between our towers, rising above the city. People were appalled, furious. All arrows pointed to him. And I said, Look, politically you're absolutely within your rights to be angry, but existentially you're wrong – *existentially* this particular poet just wants us all to be free. As a matter of fact, he's not even a poet at all, he's a phil-osopher. Yes, I said it: He's one of us. But then the poet himself said that philosophy makes nothing happen and also that he happened to quite like the Devil – whom we sometimes call 'the adversary' and sometimes nothing at all – and then he said that he was glad that he-who-shall-not-be-named had come to power, because he admired his energy, his inability to distin-guish between past, present, and future, and soon after that the poet got cancelled and, soon after that, me, too.

Grand Union

Having screamed at my six-year-old to the point that she threw herself down on her bed and wept, I felt the need to get out of the house and see my mother. She was dead, and in heaven, but for convenience's sake we met outside the chicken spot at the top of Ladbroke Grove. It was, in the moment, the blackest place I could think of. We sat together on the steps of the Golden Dragon. Mandem and galdem passed us by, heading inside for their stir-fry and their Szechuan. Mother and I regarded each other. For being dead, she looked pretty fantastic. Death could not wither her. It was merely one of a long line of things that could not wither her. She wore her dreds wrapped just right, high and impressive. Never ashy, her darkness shone. She looked the spit of Queen Nanny on the five-hundred-dollar bill.

That is not a coincidence, she said, when I mentioned the resemblance. In death, I have become Nanny of the Maroons. That is, I have always been she, but now it is revealed. Figures, I said, and she admonished me for using an Americanism and asked if I was still living in those devilish parts. I had to confess I was, but had come all this way, across an ocean, just to converse with her spirit. Well, you're Asante now, she said, and I was glad to hear it, having always suspected as much. Still, I kissed my teeth, to make clear that, like all warrior daughters,

I wanted more from my warrior mother, much more, and would never get enough. My mother kissed her teeth in turn, signifying that she understood.

Together, we surveyed the scene. All around us was carnival detritus: Red Stripe cans and abandoned yellow crusts of lamb patty and broken whistles and glittering press-on face jewellery and filthy feathers and friendly cards from the police, describing proper stop-and-search procedure, informing us of the limits of their powers. Oh, carnival! While we dance in the August sun it's wonderful, it's sticky with joy, it's the sweet flypaper of life, but then night arrives, the police hurry us home, we survey the devastated streets, we think *surely we're not going to put ourselves through all this shit again next year?* (Nanny has gone to carnival every year since 1972.) Or maybe only I think that. (The borders between me and everybody else have never been clear to me.) Maybe all cycles must be respected.

The women in our family, announced my mother, do not recognize the women in our family. Well, that seemed cheap and tautological to me so I went inside to get some chicken. Though it's a Chinese place, it empathizes with its clientele, and that day they were offering inauthentic jerk with rice and pea and two plastic forks. I watched the daughter of the establishment sigh as the mother of the establishment critiqued her Styrofoam-box-closing technique in rapid Cantonese. And I once knew a girl called Hermione whose mother would never sit down to eat. She went straight from cooking to cleaning and if anyone tried to get her to the table she said *oh, no, no, no, I'm fine with my little plate here*, and then she'd clean up after everybody and pick at that plate like a bird, one bite every half-hour or so, till it was stone cold and a skin had grown over it, at which point she'd scrape whatever was left into the bin and wash up the little plate, too. It was her way of showing love and it was so exotic to me – I was in awe of it. I went to her funeral. Seven hundred people stood up as one to chant: '*She always thought of others, never of herself!*' But you can only really know the blood you're swimming in.

When I got back outside, my mother had assumed the position of an old Obeah woman: legs wide apart, skirts falling in between, toes splayed like a duck. She still looked fantastic. Many had been the time she'd eaten the food straight off my plate before I'd even raised my plastic fork – but I could see why the Arawaks once flocked to her. If you're on the edge of extinction nothing less than Nanny will do. Yet you can't sing a note, I said to my mother – I was finally getting to the point – and the weird thing is my daughter sings with soul, truly with soul, and I suppose I'm worried about what it all means. Here my mother and all the other Obeah women in the neighbourhood paused to laugh long and loud at the way worries will sprout on wet, fertile ground yet rarely care to flower in the kind of drought conditions they themselves had known.

Now, if you asked Billie Holiday, my mother said, with her eyes closed, she would tell you: *No one sings the word 'hunger' like I do. Or the word 'love'.* That's not a defence of anything, clarified my mother, that's just a true fact. Although I'm not a Billie fan myself, daughter, as you know. Rodigan is my musical love, then, now and for ever!

I stood up. I told her I loved her. I wandered over to the Grand Union Canal which may well be that river of milk which all the daughters of the world are looking for whenever they go to the hardware store for milk, even though they know full well there's no milk at the hardware store. Hardware! Americanisms everywhere. But also love, and recognition of history, and the inconceivably broad shadow cast by the Blue Mountains, on top of which you'll find my Maroon grandfather, never dying, undead, totally undead, living eternally amongst his chickens and goats, his parcels of contested land, his dozens and dozens and dozens of out-the-house children, amongst whom a few bold girls now make their way down the shady side of the mountain, following the tread of my mudder, and her mudder, and her mudder, moving with necessary speed, not always holding each other's hands.

Acknowledgements

Tash, Devorah, Chris, Dave, Georgia, Jonathan, Ann, Dev, Cressida, Ben, Darryl and Simon all made these stories better, in one way or another. Thank you.

Thank you to Nick for reading the original 'Grand Union' and sending me on a different course, upriver.

And thanks to my mother, Yvonne, for reminding me of Kelso Cochrane at the right moment.

Permissions

Permissions

p. 189: 'A Humanist View' by Toni Morrison, delivered at Portland State University's Oregon Public Speakers Collection, 'Black Studies Center public dialogue, Part II', 30 May 1975.

p. 195: Patrick Digby quoted in the *Daily Express*, 21 May 1959 (Headline: YOUTHS GO HOME AFTER 50 HOURS). Evidence of Patrick Digby's involvement in Kelso Cochrane's murder, along with other details of the case, are outlined in Mark Olden's *Murder in Notting Hill* (Zero Books, 2011).

p. 196: Francis Ponge, *La Table*, © Éditions Gallimard.

p. 197: Paul Gilroy, *Between Camps: Nations, Cultures and the Allure of Race* (Routledge UK, 2004) and *Against Race: Imagining Political Culture Beyond the Color Line* (Belknap Press of Harvard University Press, 2000).

Acknowledgement is also due to the following publications, in which some of these stories first appeared:

'The Lazy River' was first published in the *New Yorker*, 18 December 2017.

'Just Right' was first published in *Granta* magazine, 6 April 2013.

'Miss Adele Amidst the Corsets' was first published in the *Paris Review*, Spring 2014.

'Escape from New York' was first published in the *New Yorker*, 8 June 2015.

'Big Week' was first published in the *Paris Review*, Summer 2014.

'Meet the President!' was first published in the *New Yorker*, 12 August 2013.

'Two Men Arrive in a Village' was first published in the *New Yorker*, 6 June 2016.

'Now More Than Ever' was first published in the *New Yorker*, 23 July 2018.